April 16
8:17 P.M.

I remember once when Melanie, Cam, Meg, Angelica, and I were watching a Miss America contest at Angelica's, and helping Angelica's mother pack some boxes to send to a third world country that had just had a devastating flood. We thought that many of the contestants seemed pretty broad in the beam! Maybe that is because pictures can put on five or so pounds. We all decided that we did not want to be as fat as they were when we got to be their age!

Mrs. Garrito brought out some snacks and I hated myself for scarfing down everything edible. I wonder if anyone else feels like I do? A big fraud for talking about wanting to be thin . . . and then eating like I was part of the third world starvation situation. I despise myself for being so undisciplined! I really do! I feel like I'm a wimpy, insipid, unworthy, whatever!

Other books edited by
BEATRICE SPARKS, PH.D.

TREACHEROUS LOVE

ALMOST LOST

ANNIE'S BABY

IT HAPPENED TO NANCY

Kim: empty inside

The Diary of an Anonymous Teenager

Edited by Beatrice Sparks, Ph.D.

AVON BOOKS
An Imprint of HarperCollins Publishers

Library of Congress Cataloging-in-Publication Data
Sparks, Beatrice.
  Kim : empty inside / edited [i.e. written] by Beatrice Sparks.
     p.   cm.
  Summary: Seventeen-year-old Kim, feeling the pressure of maintaining an A average
to stay on her college gymnastics team, becomes obsessive about her weight and
develops anorexia.
  ISBN 0-380-81460-9 (pbk.)
  [1. Anorexia nervosa—Fiction. 2. Weight control—Fiction. 3. Gymnastics—Fiction.
4. Universities and colleges—Fiction. 5. Diaries—Fiction.] I. Title.
PZ7.S737135 Ki 2002   2001039372
[Fic]—dc21   CIP
                                                                              AC

First Avon edition, 2002

To Kimberly and every other young

person who wanders through the

scary maze of an eating disorder.

Your journey may seem confusing,

complicated, sometimes even sinister.

But you *can* find your way out!

You are not alone.

Kim: empty inside

March 1

Wow! Today Melanie and I were checking out things we couldn't afford in the mall, when she spotted a little table stacked with journals. Neither of us had had one since we were little kids. Then they were called diaries and they were a third the size of these journals and a third as thick. It will be fun next year, when I am in college, to read about my last year in high school. Going from a diary to a journal is like exploding into adulthood. SCARY.

March 2

Nothing much happens in my dull life in Arizona . . . SAME OLD SAME OLD . . . Except next month we should be getting our college acceptances. IF we are accepted! I'm not absolutely, positively sure I WANT to go away from my family and friends and . . . everything in the world I know. Imagine seventeen-year-old me at a huge university.

March 6, Tuesday

I hurt my wrist on a floor exercise today. I don't know how or when it happened . . . which is weird . . . it didn't really start hurting bad till I'd finished my routine. Gymnasts are used to living with pain but wow. I'm home now using hot and cold compresses. Lucky it's my left wrist so I can write. Melanie and I had planned on going to the library, but she insisted I stay home and take care of my wrist. We girls on the team really try to encourage and work with each other. Our coach, Miss Muskinko, insists on that, and we trust her.

5:35 P.M.

Melanie probably called Cam as soon as I hung up and now they are at the library looking for guys. And I'm not. It's amazing how many guys there are that WE would like to be magnets for, and how few . . . like practically none . . . seem attracted to us. Melanie and I can talk to each other about almost anything, like really wanting . . . almost physically longing for . . . some nice, handsome, smart, male person to hold our hand . . . put his arm around our shoulders or . . . just to let us know we are . . . human female creatures that need human male creatures. I don't mean needing us just as sexual objects, like the gross guys that make you want to throw up when they touch you. We can't figure out how about five percent of the girls get about ninety-five percent of the guys. I read in a magazine that that is what happens! It's not fair and IT'S NOT RIGHT! BUT THAT'S THE WAY IT IS! GUYS GET ALL THE BREAKS! Or do they? Maybe I'm just a dumb naive kid who wants to be a princess.

6:45 P.M.

Is it normal to be jealous of girls who have boyfriends? I don't mean friends like Tad and Josh and Will, who treat us like we're . . . a sister or cousin or something. I don't want to be a sister or cousin!

7:32 P.M.

Just as I was thinking . . . and feeling myself dancing in Tad's arms . . . with him looking deep into my eyes like I WAS someone very close and special, the stupid phone rang. So much for that! Wrong number!

Once when I was about thirteen, when we were still living in North Carolina, my friend Katie and I went to the Magic Shop on Fourth Street and bought some perfume that was supposed to draw guys like flies. It didn't work, nor did the candles and the other dumb stuff we got. Were we desperate? I still am!

It was really hard for me when we moved here. Dad had been offered a job on the hospital staff, with all kinds of perks, and Mom had been given a not-too-demanding job in accounting (which she loved). Dara and Lara, my twin sisters, had each other! Dara and Lara were eleven when I was born so they had always had each other. I envied them! Mom and Dad were like one entity they had been married so long . . . AND ME? Nada as usual! I wish the twins were teaching here instead of halfway across the nation. I miss them like part of me is gone. Sometimes I

3

think I'm the only one in the world who doesn't have somebody.

That's dumb!

9:46 P.M.

I've been thinking of asking Mom to let me stop taking piano lessons, but when I walked by the piano with my left arm wrapped in its bulky cold compress, I realized how much I'd miss playing. I really love music and gymnastics and all the other stuff I sometimes think I don't like. SOOOOOOO . . . I'm a . . . Sometimes I don't know who . . . or what . . . I am.

March 15, Thursday

My arm is getting better but Miss Muskinko told me to take a little more time off. I had to watch everyone else doing the things I wanted to be doing on floor and bars and beams. Miss Muskinko suggested I scrutinize each person carefully and try to sense, as well as see, what they were doing right and wrong. She said I could learn a lot that way. It worked! In fact, I felt kind of like a COACH myself. I'm dedicated to gymnastics. I have been since the first day I was introduced to it in seventh grade. Even then it gave me a thrill and a boost that I can't get any other way! It's like defying gravity or something.

I WONDER . . . If I were lighter . . . could I fly higher? Ummmmmmm, what's to lose? A pound or two—or ten? No! Not ten!

4

March 16

A small group of us have been working our hearts out getting ready for the "SPRING THING." That's a crazy name for a dance, but we all went along with the idea. Tonight it finally came!

The gym was decorated like a great garden, with hundreds of paper flowers, and the music was sometimes sweet, sometimes hectic. Usually hectic because the teachers don't want the couples to get, well, *too* together.

I danced a lot and I think had more fun than I've ever had. I probably even sweated off a few totally grotesque pounds . . . ummmmm, wouldn't that be nice.

I danced with Tad a lot. We'd worked together on the Spring Thing committee. Then dorky Dick Miller asked me to dance. I really didn't want to—no way! no how! But I said yes anyway. Mom would be proud if I told her, because it was NOT easy!

March 22

Wonderful, wonderful day! Tad called and asked if I wanted to go with him to a movie tonight. Did I want to go? I wanted to so badly I'd have climbed through the telephone lines to get to him.

Tad said he liked my shoulder-length hair pulled up in tight curls and my pink pants and tank top, which I had thought looked kind of babyish and made me look fat. He said they looked like spring, or maybe an early, early sunrise or a late, late sunset. Then he gently touched the tank top fabric and said it felt as soft and ethereal as it looked. I felt SPECIAL! It was a feeling too grandiose and tender for words.

We saw *All the Pretty Horses*. It was lame, but it gave us lots to laugh about at the Burger Bin and on the way home. I've never had many real dates in my life . . . two, to be exact . . . and they were both kind of, well . . . uncomfortable. Being with Tad tonight was like . . . warm and fuzzy, not kissy, but not sister or cousinish either. I hope we have lots more time together!!!

I thought I looked fat and frumpy but he thought I looked cool. I hope he wasn't just saying that!

I have to go with my parents this weekend to visit Dad's cousin, who is sick. I hope Tad doesn't lose interest in me while I'm gone. That is, if he ever was really interested, and not just asking me out because there was nothing else to do.

March 23

It's spooky waiting to see if I'll be accepted at UCLA, my first choice! I'm barely seventeen . . . well, seventeen and one-half. My parents let me skip a grade—actually, almost a grade and a half—when I was nine. I asked Mom about it once when I was in middle school, and most all the girls were getting boobs except me. I stuffed cotton in my training bra every day. Mom said my teacher had insisted that I was completely bored and mentally beyond what she was teaching. She felt I was an extremely bright child, and I might begin to resent school. I remember I didn't like school too much for a while, but now I love it . . . well, most of the time.

March 24
Dumb, dull day visiting Dad's cousin.

March 28
Tad is a brain and he wants to go to Harvard. But he's not positively sure he will be accepted even though his dad went there.

This sounds terrible, I know . . . but I don't want him to be accepted at Harvard! He's applied to a number of schools and UCLA IS ONE OF THEM! That is where my heart tells me he should go. If only wishes really came true like in fairy tales!!!

9:43 P.M.
College acceptance letters are supposed to come in APRIL. What if I don't get one? What if I do?

April 4, Wednesday
Happiest day of all HAPPY DAYS IN THE WORLD! I received my acceptance letter from UCLA! I found it when I got home from school. I called Mom's office but she was in a meeting. Dad was in surgery. I tried my sisters' cell phones but couldn't reach either of them, guess they were teaching classes.

Desperate, I tried to call both Melanie and Cam and couldn't get either of them.

6:57 P.M.

I felt like I was about to explode with anticipation when I heard Mom's key in the door. I held up the letter and she bounced around like a teenager, happy as I was—happier, if possible! When Dad came in he was wilder than both Mom and me put together.

Mom graduated from UCLA, as did Lara and Dara, and all my life I'd heard fantastic stories about it: sororities and parties and games and all the exciting and marvelous intellectual things that go on in college. And now it's going to be MY turn! Mom had to reassure me that it WAS my name on the letter and that they hadn't made a mistake.

We went out to dinner at Cowboy Jack's Steak House to celebrate and I ate my part of the cow, and then some! Mom and Dad laughed at me, and with me, and it was like they were, for a while, my friends instead of my parents. I can diet . . . on regular days!

SUPER FUN TIME!!!!

11:42 P.M.

After dinner I called Dara and Lara and FINALLY got them on the line. We joked and bawled at the same time, me scared of going away and them trying to say Mom and Dad would be glad to get rid of me. They said what I really needed was to come live with them and go to the school where they teach. "Fat chance," I said. "Then I'd have two extra moms to nag at me!" We talked for ever and ever!

I tremendously appreciate the telephone. I don't know what I'd do without it. I just close my eyes and it's like whoever is talking is right there with me.

April 5
12:41 A.M.

Now that the time is really getting close for me to go away to college (September 28) I'm not positively sure I should go. I'm young, and more than that I suspect I'm kind of immature. Will I be able to cut it? If I can't, then what? And what about Tad? Maybe I should wait until next year or go to junior college here. I'll talk to Mom and Dad about it in the morning. I KNOW I WON'T . . . BUT MAYBE . . . I WILL . . . NO!!! Positively I won't!

Instead . . .

I'll go check out the refrigerator

and

the cookie jar.

FOOD IS MY FRIEND!

6:42 P.M.

After school Cam and Melanie and I met Tad and Jake at the mall. We hung out for a while, then Jake looked at his watch and jumped up, saying he had his mom's car and had to bring it home. Tad patted my shoulder as he passed and it

9

was like an electric shock going through my body. I know that sounds dumb but . . . it did feel like that. It really did!

Cam had to dash home to baby-sit, and so Melanie and I had some quiet time to ourselves. We walked down to the White Rock Well and sat on a bench in the shade. I DIDN'T want to talk about Tad but words started spouting out of my mouth anyway. Why hadn't he telephoned? Why hadn't he asked me out again? Why?????

Melanie started on a chain of answers.

Probably he was working hard on his college entry stuff . . .

Maybe his car was in the garage . . .

His mom wouldn't let him use her car . . .

He was saving his money . . . etc., etc., etc.

I hope those things are right! I know Tad is totally dedicated to everything he does and probably he is overwhelmingly busy helping his mom—since his dad left—and, on top of that, getting things put together to go to college. He also works with troubled middle school kids. I can't remember what the group is called. I'M PROUD OF TAD! He's out spending his time doing good while I'm just feeling sorry for myself. I've got to be more patient and understanding. I know he likes me!!!!! That is enough for now . . . not really . . . but . . .

I feel a little better now.

11:21 P.M.

I just had the most wonderful dream about Tad and me. We were both at Harvard and completely depending upon each other. I know Tad applied there; I don't know why I didn't. I guess because Mom and the twins had me so psyched up about UCLA. I wonder what would have happened if . . .

Good night, sweet Tad. I'm going to try to go back to sleep and dream about you some more.

April 7, Saturday

Melanie, Cam, Susan (Cam's cousin), and I worked at a nursing home most of the day. We sang, played games with them, listened to some people's absolutely astounding stories as well as some of their dry, dull, went-on-forever meanderings.

It was an interesting and completely different kind of experience.

—STILL—

WE'VE ALL DECIDED WE DON'T WANT TO GET OLD!!!! EVER!!!!!

We're going to start eating more nourishing food, exercising, being less uptight and worried, etc. We've also got our own motto: HAVE I DONE ANY GOOD IN THE WORLD TODAY?

April 9

I guess by now its pretty obvious that Tad didn't feel as much for me as I felt for him. I hope we're still friends, but beyond that, I guess . . . nada, zero, zilch. Maybe if I was prettier, or brighter, or nicer, or THINNER . . . probably thinner!

I'm always looking for Tad in the halls . . . but he's become invisible.

I've talked to my friends, at least Cam and Melanie, but they are as stupidly naive about how to handle things like . . . young male entities! . . . as I am.

Sometimes life seems like . . . not worth the effort! And I certainly don't want to make a fool of myself by chasing him.

April 12
9:17 P.M.
NEW TIME!
NEW LIFE!

I'm trying to be more mature . . . that's a laugh! We're all going in different directions. Cam will be going to junior college here in town and Melanie will be going to . . . I've forgotten the name of the school but it's back east and not very well known, but it's supposed to be good and it's cheaper than most. Her folks don't have very much money. Sometimes I don't appreciate that my dad is a doctor.

10:39 P.M.

It seems that fall will be here tomorrow. I wish I could hold it back for a long, long time. Or do I? I want to get out of my house this minute! I'm tired of being treated like I don't know which way is up! Still, sometimes I have nightmares of being a complete loner in a crummy sorority house—a fat, boyfriendless loner, shunned by every breathing creature. I'm like a stupid yo-yo.

I hope someday I can find a strong man like my dad to keep me on an even keel. What if I fall for some gorgeous hunk with not a brain in his head? THAT won't happen because I'm more attracted to interiors than exteriors . . . I think . . . I hope . . .

April 13, Good Friday

It is really a GOOD FRIDAY—IN FACT, A FABULOUS FRIDAY! I've pinched myself until I'm going to have black-and-blue marks all over my body! Can this really be true? Oh, I hope, hope, hope I'm not dreaming!

Miss Muskinko, our coach, called me into her office, and she was more excited than I've ever seen her before. She told me that a few weeks ago she sent some tapes of me to a gymnastic coach at UCLA. The UCLA coach called to say I appeared to have a lot of natural ability and she would be looking forward to seeing me in person.

THIS IS SCARY! WONDERFUL BUT SCARY!

I'm wondering if I'm dedicated enough to be on a really great team. I know SOMETIMES I amaze myself, but . . . most of the time I'm . . . lazy? . . . Maybe not devoted? Would I be willing, or able, to give my all?

I was soooooo excited I had to cut Social Studies class to call Mom and Dad. They weren't even mad at me and Dad turned the patient he was seeing over to another doctor so he could hear every detail. And Mom said she almost jumped on top of her desk to dance.

If I do make the team it won't be for some time because they will want to judge me in person! Alone! That's terrifying!

April 14, Saturday

Mom and Dad took off this afternoon and we drove up to Indian Waters. It was almost like I was going to leave for UCLA tomorrow, instead of in five months. Dad rented a sailboat and we flipped around the little lake almost as if we owned it. Mom got scared a few times because Dad did get a little show-offish. But I loved it! It was an invigorating and dangerous feeling! I didn't want it to ever end. Something inside me doesn't want to ever go away from my family, while another part of me can't wait to get away. I know that's stupid, but that's the way it is!

The sunset looked like some giant kid up in the sky had spilled his watercolors. Blue and orange and yellow and red hues dripped and sloshed over the horizon. It was one of the most beautiful scenes I have ever seen and it will be forever painted in my mind.

Now to the gross part. I'm embarrassed to even write this . . . but it happened! We went to the Lodge for dinner and ordered about everything on the menu. We were so hungry from our boating and hiking. While we were eating Dad saw one of his doctor friends and his wife come in. He and Mom rushed over to meet them, which left me at the table by myself. I looked down at the food on my plate and suddenly realized it was ALL FAT, FAT, FAT, greasy, uncooked white pig fat. I could picture myself eating it and the fat blubbering out of every pore in my body and I about threw up right there. Very plainly I could see myself on the bars and the beam and the floor . . . fat as the fat lady in the circus, trying to do my routines . . . and making a complete, laughable fool out of myself! I scooped my pork chop and practically everything else up in my napkin and poked it behind a potted plant. I left just a few veggies to push around on the plate when my folks got back. I HAVE NO IDEA WHY I DO IDIOTIC THINGS LIKE THAT . . .

Except . . . I've worked for years to be physically fit and there is no way I'm going to let myself balloon out now! NOW, when maybe . . . I might possibly . . . get on the UCLA gymnastics team.

We got home at 9:00 and we all went straight to bed.

April 15
1:33 A.M.
My growling stomach woke me up a few minutes ago and my first inclination was to dash to the kitchen, but I resisted! I hadn't had much lunch, I'd dumped my dinner, and we'd hiked for six or seven miles, so I should have shed a little repulsiveness. I'm certainly NOT going to plaster it back on! A bottle of flavored water should take care of the tummy thing.

April 15, Easter Sunday

Melanie, Cam, and I spent the whole day just goofing off, at Cam's house, then at mine. We talked about being little and looking for Easter eggs and stuff, then about leaving home for college and how scary it would be . . . but how great and free, too! Cam didn't have to worry so much because she will be staying right here, living at home and going to junior college. Maybe she's lucky, but maybe not! It's hard to predict the future. Then we started talking about guys, guys, guys! That sparked things up a bit, but only in our dreams. All three of us are duds. Oh, Cam had a REAL boyfriend once, but he turned out to be a jerk after the first few dates, wanting all or nothing at all. We about laughed ourselves to death on that, because none of us know what we're talking about or what we really want.

P.S. I wouldn't . . . couldn't . . . tell Melanie or Cam this, but what I REALLY WANT IS TAD!

April 16

I've been working my heart out in gymnastics and classes! UCLA is expensive and demanding. I guess I'm lucky. In a way it's good; in another way, it is possibly more responsibility than I can reasonably handle . . . because I'm basically a goof-off a lot of the time. I hope I'm not making a mistake that will ruin my life! My parents would be crushed if I didn't make the grade and my sisters would be humiliated and uncomfortable around me forever. I've got to make it!!!! I'VE REALLY GOT TO!!! Laurie Longden won all kinds of medals and honors before she became a UCLA coach. I'm sure I'll never be THAT good, but maybe I could be a coach in a little junior college or something. I've never been able to figure out WHAT I want to do . . . or be . . . when I've actually grown up! I'm not even sure that I want to ever grow up! Dumb! Childish, huh? Yep, that's me!

8:17 P.M.

I am so ashamed of hiding my food behind the plant at Indian Waters. I can't believe I do such ridiculous things! Melanie and Cam and I often talk about not wanting to be fat, but then everybody talks that way! Even girls in grade school. They just don't get into the deep-fat crazies like I do . . . watching blobs of blubber pop out on my thighs and hips like they were mushrooms after a rainstorm . . . uggggh.

I remember once when Melanie, Cam, Meg, Angelica, and I were watching a Miss America contest at Angelica's, and helping Angelica's mother pack some boxes to send to a third world country that had just had a devastating flood. We thought that many of the contestants seemed pretty broad in the beam! Maybe that is because pictures can put on five or so pounds. I read that somewhere. We all decided that we did not want to be as fat as they were when we got to be their age! And we went back to packing boxes.

Some of the boxes were heavy, heavy, heavy. Angelica's mom said she should have invited a few football players.

Melanie, Cam, Angelica, and I jumped up and shouted, "It's not too late! Invite them! INVITE THEM!" We stooped over like our backs were killing us and pretended we couldn't even make our hands work. Mrs. Garrito just smiled and shook her head. "Silly, silly, boy-struck girls," she said, laughing. "I remember when I was your age. Oh, do I remember!" She had a smile on her face that made us wonder WHAT she was remembering! None of us had had any out-of-this-world-exciting experiences that would bring smiles to our faces like hers!

We talked for a long time about what was wrong with us. Were we mutants of some kind that couldn't attract a bear if we were doused with honey? And on and on until we were all on the floor rolling with laughter.

Mrs. Garrito brought out some snacks and I hated myself for scarfing down everything edible. I wonder if anyone else feels like I do? A big fraud for talking about wanting to be thin . . . and then eating like I was part of the third world starvation situation. I despise myself for being so undisciplined! I really do! I feel like I'm a wimpy, insipid, unworthy, whatever!

11:32 P.M.
Mom called to say they would be late. How late is "late"? They went out to dinner with some people they work with, and I'm left here alone in this big, big, old, old, cold, cold, ugly, unfriendly apartment. Six stories up, with not a real tree in

sight in any direction. I hate it, hate it, HATE IT!

We've been here almost a year and I miss our old *real home* with the big green grassy yard and all the flowers, and the goldfish pond, and our swing that reached almost up to the sky when someone pushed you hard enough! I was BORN there. It was REAL! This place is like the ant house I used to have, with people, instead of ants, scattering and scampering up and down in every other direction.

Sometimes I think I'll die I miss Dara and Lara sooooo much! They babied me and spoiled me and dragged me around with them like I was a little puppy or something. I remember one night when I had an earache and I went from Lara's bed to Dara's bed through the whole night. They cuddled me and rubbed around my ear and kissed it better. I'm sure that healed it more than Dr. Dad's eardrops.

One time when I told Melanie that Dara and Lara were eleven years old when I was born, she asked me if they seemed like my mom and my mom seemed like my grandmother. I laughed so hard I almost choked to death.

April 17
12:25 A.M.

Mom and Dad just came in. I pretended I was asleep. I didn't want to listen to them tell me what wonderful lives they have and how important they are.

12:55 A.M.

I can't seem to go to sleep for some crazy reason. How can I be so cold and lonely? Why couldn't I have been born a twin? Lara and Dara were never lonely. Only me.

Garbage! I'm just selfish and self-centered!

I want to go back home. Back to my old, comfortable, pastel, real home. I want to be able to stretch out on the grass under the big trees and get muddy in the pond, have a yard and privacy and not a snooty doorman, and everybody trying to impress everybody else. Why did we ever . . .

ever . . .

ever . . . have to move away from everything softly comforting and natural and beautiful? Will I ever adjust? Will I ever, ever get used to my ugly, ugly, ugly, cold, cold, cold, new abode? Our apartment is big but it's all gray and brown and totally ugly.

Day? Who knows? Who cares?

I'm really bummed out after having had bad dreams all night. I barely existed through my morning classes, my heart filled with fear that Melanie had found another . . . a . . . better friend. Like in my dream. Thank goodness she hadn't. She was waiting for me by the front door. We whispered as we sat on the steps. I told her about my ghastly dream—no! Nightmare! Melanie talked me down, and the loving things she said were like soothing music to my heart. It made me see everything, including the school, in a completely different light. It's a beautiful school, old but well kept. Everything is clean, what lawns they have are green and trimmed. We walked completely around the building, then up to the third floor. As we hurried down the stairs at the sound of the first bell, we both gave the place an overall A+. Melanie drawled, "It's all we've got; we'd better like it."

"I like it." I grinned. "And I like you . . . a lot."

I'm a little embarrassed about saying that. I hope it didn't sound like . . . I'm desperate for a friend or anything like that.

5:59 P.M.

I hate coming back to our cold, old, high-in-the-sky—whatever. It's like we're stacked on shelves in a grocery store. Everything is so blaaah I'm beginning to see myself that way too.

Our building, the Regency, has a luxurious restaurant on the ground floor, and Mom and Dad said I could go there anytime I want and order what I want, then just sign the check, but . . . that's not what I need. I need them!

But they're up to their eyebrows in hospital and medical school problems. I've got to be more patient and understanding. I heard them talking one night about the horrible way the med school was run just before they came and what a challenge it would be to get it back to the respectable place it used to be. How they'd had no idea the place would be in such an awful condition. Oh, well . . . I guess I

21

should just be glad I'm not part of that problem—AND I DO HAVE MELANIE and CAM.

And the refrigerator . . . it's my security blanket.

April 20
6:00 A.M.

Mom and Dad woke me out of a sound sleep. It about scared me to death because I thought something had happened to Lara or Dara. But it hadn't. Actually, a fire had started in the furnace room in the college where they teach. There wasn't major damage done, but it would still take four or five days to get things cleaned up, and school would be closed for that time.

Dara and Lara had called and begged Mom and Dad to let me take four days off and come visit them. The twins wanted me to leave on the next plane, and Mom and Dad said yes.

Wow! Friday, Saturday, Sunday, and Monday! UN-BELIEVABLE!

I guess my last e-mail to the twins made it seem like I hated it here and was more terminally unhappy than I really am.

Thank goodness my parents know I'm a good student and that I can catch up on two missed school days with no sweat. I know they feel very guilty because they're gone so much, but they shouldn't. They can't help it, and it won't last forever—although it feels like forever!

Mom is taking me to the airport in a few minutes. I can't believe this wonderful thing is happening to me! And I've simply got to stop being so negative. Eventually, Mom will have a regular work schedule. Maybe then we can get some color in this spooky, cold, dark apartment. But that's ME! A spoiled brat.

I wonder if the twins miss me as much as I miss them! I doubt it!

April 23
This weekend has been so much fun!

Lara and Dara have a cute little cottage kind of house with trees and grass, and I love it, love it, love it! I didn't dare tell them that I secretly wanted to stay and live with them! I knew that wouldn't work. NO WAY! First of all, Mom and Dad wouldn't like it, and secondly both twins have boyfriends—in fact, they teased each other about soon being "old married ladies." I didn't meet the guys. Lara and Dara said they wanted this weekend to be just for me. And I really do want to go to UCLA.

I'm happy for them . . . sad for me . . . well, not really sad but . . . I don't know, maybe I'm just selfish and I'm afraid they'll love their husbands more than me. Dumb, huh?

Their pretty Lilliputian house has two bedrooms but they are so teeny-tiny that they've each chosen to have a twin bed so they can have fairly large desks with computers and stuff.

The first night I shifted from Lara's bed to Dara's. A

TWIN BED IS SO SMALL that two people in one bed hang over on both sides. We giggled and nagged and by the second night took turns sleeping on the floor, which was a lot more comfortable!

From the moment we woke up till late, late at night, they were taking me places and showing me things. I can see why they chose to come teach here. It's a great place for them . . . but I don't know about for me.

When I said that, Dara pulled my ear and snarled that if I did come there she'd probably be my mean old teacher and that she'd take care of "spoiled brat little squirty me."

We all broke out laughing at that and started a three-way wrestling match like we used to have when I was little and when they came home on vacations.

I didn't want to leave!

When the twins took me to the airport to come home we blubbered and cried and laughed and teased until people around us were watching, but we didn't care. They weren't acting like serious schoolteachers. They were acting like . . . my goofy sisters!

Before I left they made me promise—on our family's silly old Solemn Promise Oath: Cross my heart, etc.—that I'd stay clean and sober, and I promised gladly. I want to be like them! They're my idols, my mentors, my sisters!

I felt so disconnected I cried almost all the way home in the plane. The flight attendant kept coming by to offer me stuff and asking me if I was all right. It was embarrassing, but I still couldn't stop crying. Partly I was crying from happiness, and that didn't make any sense at all.

11:45 P.M.

I feel like I'm in some kind of a twilight zone. Mom and Dad picked me up at the airport at 9:20 P.M. and they were like two little kids they were so happy to see me. They said the apartment had been cold and lonely and QUIET, QUIET, QUIET! with me gone.

People stared at us like we were crazy, but we didn't care. Even Dad, who has always been so formal and staid in public, didn't care!

On the way home Mom and Dad wanted to know every detail about Dara and Lara, and squashed between them in the front seat I could feel how much they loved the three of us. Dad and Mom have their own lives . . . but we come first. It was something I had never known before, how lovely it is to be loved so deeply!

When we got to the Regency, Mom couldn't help giggling and I knew there must be some kind of surprise for me. But what?

When we got out of the elevator on our floor Dad pulled a silk scarf out of his pocket and blindfolded me.

By the time we walked through the entry and into the great room, I was about to explode! I could smell pine scent coming from the fireplace and the fragrance of flowers was like a warm hug.

When Dad took off the blindfold I WAS BACK IN MY OLD HOME! . . . well, almost. The wall colors and the drapes were the same barely yellow sunset colors and the furniture was huge, pastel, soft and inviting. Two large live trees flanked the huge picture window that gives us a view of the city and Red Hill. Potted plants were everywhere. Mom loves flowers and now she had more than the one little scrawny geranium she'd brought with us.

When I saw my room, it was almost too wonderful to bear. IT WAS MY OLD ROOM! Well, almost: the bed, the colors, the chest, the carpet, even the two little white canaries in a tall white cage . . . I started crying . . . I was in heaven. I'd hated it when they sold our house furnished!

Mom made me promise I wouldn't tell the twins. I'm such a motormouth . . . I hope I can keep the secret. Their room (the guest room) is huge and totally yummy! Maybe they'll love it so much they'll transfer from their school here. But I'd better not get my hopes up. Besides, I'll be away at college myself.

Mom had taken off work while I was gone and about killed herself getting things done. Even Dad had taken time off to help buy the furniture. They're really the greatest and the most thoughtful and . . . well . . . the kind of parents every kid should have!

April 24

Melanie was as happy to see me as I was to see her. We had so much to tell each other that we were both talking and laughing at the same time. It was like we had been apart for years, not days.

A new boy has moved into Melanie's building. She says that to him she's just another Dust Bunny, but she still likes to pretend he's crazy about her.

I told her I thought she was just plain crazy, and we laughed so hard by our lockers that everyone thought we both were crazy.

In a way, Melanie fills in for the twins. They leave a big empty hole in my life after every time I see them.

May 3

Cam and I spent most of the late afternoon at the mall—eating, shopping, eating again, going to a movie, and eating *again*. Then both of us had to upchuck in the ladies room. I hope she isn't as food fetishy as I am.

Cam's sleeping over because her mom went on a business trip with her dad. I'm really, really happy and thankful that she and Melanie are my best friends.

May 4

At breakfast Dad told Cam and me about a beautiful little four-year-old girl whose heart had been in backward or something and how he had operated and fixed her up so she'd have a normal life.

It made us both very grateful for our own health and we've decided to think about becoming either nurses or doctors. We could even go to the same medical school and be a team. Maybe Melanie will go with us.

I was sad when Cam had to go home. I wish we were twins. I've always envied Lara and Dara. There's something about twins that's different.

May 7
Today in History we saw a film on pioneers. I think I would have liked living in those times—growing your own food and riding horses and reading by candlelight . . . but then again . . . probably NOT! DEFINITELY NOT! I think I appreciate luxuries: hot baths, gas heat, grocery stores, cars, malls, lots of pairs of cool shoes, etc.

May 8
Met Melanie and Cam at the mall. We bummed around for a while talking about how cool it was to be getting out of our cages. Then we went to McDonald's for a snack. Bret and Joey came in and joined us, and we started dissing the school cafeteria food. Bret is really funny and he's supercute. The only problem is I think Melanie likes him too.

5:22 P.M.
Wow! Can you believe this? Bret just called and asked me to go with him to a concert. The HEAD BANGERS AND MERRY MARY. I thought Bret liked Melanie. I hope he didn't ask me just to make her jealous.

Ummmm, I know Melanie likes Bret! I wonder if she'll drop me if I go out with him. I couldn't handle that. I need her friendship. Oh, crap, isn't life difficult?

I finally had to call Melanie to find out exactly what was happening. Not that I'd ask her point-blank . . . about anything. I needn't have worried because the minute she heard my voice she started talking so fast and ramblingly that it was hard for me to make any sense out of her words—Nicky, Nicky, Nicky! Finally I got the drift that Nicky was a guy (not a girl) and he had asked her to go to a movie. I was so glad, my heart about leapt out of my body. Melanie kept telling me how cool Nicky was and how she'd known him in middle school and on and on. I didn't tell her anything about Bret. I'll just drop it lightly sometime like it was nothing. NOTHING! I hadn't had a boy look at me in forever. Now my problem is to get Mom to let me go to the concert!

May 11
The Head Bangers and Merry Mary concert wasn't nearly as good as I thought it would be, and Bret is . . . weird . . . at least semiweird.

May 12
Bret seems to like me a lot, but he's kind of a pain too. He can't understand that my gymnastics time and study time are important to me and that I'm really not ready for . . . I don't know!

29

May 14

Bret stalks me in the mall and calls me every night and wants to see me every day. It's like he wants to own me, and I've only had one real date with him. In a way, I'm almost afraid of him! Stupid and childish, huh?

Melanie and I have decided it's almost better to have no boyfriend at all than to have one who's too possessive. She's lucky Nicky isn't like that.

Bret totally ruined Mother's Day, calling me three times and dropping by while we were having dinner in the Regency Royal Room. Mom and Dad thought he was nice but, ummm . . . little do they know!

May 16

Bret drove by as Melanie and I were waiting to catch our bus home from school. He stopped and offered me a ride. I told him I was going to Melanie's (which wasn't really true, but I didn't want to go with him).

The guy who was with Bret opened the door on his side and grabbed Melanie's arm. "Red can go with me," he said.

Melanie pulled away and we both started running toward Jody's mother's car. We could smell that the guys had been drinking.

"Who needs you bitches," Bret and his friend called back to us as they gunned down the street.

When we got close to Jody's mother's car, Melanie held my hand and shivered. "I'm sorry I was jealous of you when Bret was following you around like a sick puppy," she said.

I shrugged. "I had no idea he was soooo . . ." I had no words.

Melanie snickered. "Compared to Bret, Nicky is a skinny little wimp, but he's safe . . . I think I'll take safe!"

Walking close together, we hurried to the phone and called Mom to pick us up.

"What will we tell her?" Melanie asked.

"Anything BUT the truth," I said, trying to lift our spirits.

May 17

Can you believe this! Coach Muskinko called just minutes after I'd come into the house. She said she had MORE NEWS that was SO GOOD it couldn't wait until tomorrow. The UCLA coaches have been looking over tapes and want to encourage me to continue practicing! practicing! practicing! They're looking forward to meeting me. I thought I'd faint or maybe die right there with the phone in my hand . . . but I didn't!

"Me? Me?" I kept asking. Miss Muskinko laughed and I laughed with her. Imagine ME having any kind of chance! I can't wait for Mom to get home so I can tell her.

Called Mom but she'd just left for a meeting. I had to talk to someone, so I called Melanie. She was almost as thrilled as I am, and we talked about gymnastics and going to college and stuff for a couple of hours. It was scary in one way and wondrous in another. Being on our own . . . no parents to tell us when to breathe in and when to breathe out, no lectures, no nagging about cleaning up our rooms, etc., etc., etc. Then we talked about the good things about our parents and we both cried like babies and decided we DIDN'T want to leave ever! Unless we could go together and be roommates, which of course we can't because she's not going to UCLA. I can't believe I'm that grown-up! I don't feel grown-up!

May 18
Cam and I are going to do something together today. I'm glad, because Melanie and Nicky have become like clones.

May 19
I've become almost obsessed by gymnastics. I've GOT to get on the UCLA team. That will be my way of becoming a something, a somebody! Mom and Dad will be proud of me, and everybody will want to be my friend! Glory, Glory Hallelujah!

May 21
Today I was a mess. I did a flip on the bars and came down on my upper back in such a way I thought I'd never get up. I soaked in the hot tub until I was waterlogged and my skin was all wrinkly. Sometimes I wonder if the gain is really worth the pain.
IT IS!

May 23

I can't believe I feel so good today, when for the last two days I felt so physically banged up and mentally low I could have crawled under rocks.

9:43 P.M.

We're having our last gymnastics meet Saturday. I've GOT to make a good showing . . . for our school . . . for our town . . . for UCLA! . . . for my mom and dad and sisters . . .

Then GRADUATION! In many ways I've tried not to dwell on it! There is something about graduating that is SCARY! Like crossing the Grand Canyon . . .

May 24

What a busy day! Helped Ms. Cameron put some papers away and clean out a lot of junk stuff, then went down to the gym to help set up for the BARN DANCE tomorrow night. I hope it's not a corny fiasco. Probably not though, with Tad in charge. (We're still friends. I WISH WE WERE MORE! I REALLY REALLY WISH WE WERE MORE!!!)

Tad and I, along with the rest of our committee, have set up an old-fashioned country party with line-dancing and karaoke. I didn't like the idea at first but now I think it's going to be fun. Tad is the most innovative, ambitious, artistic person alive, and the thing couldn't have been put together without him.

I like him so much it hurts and . . . I'm grateful that we're still friends. Maybe his hormones haven't kicked in yet, even though he's eighteen. And I DO REALIZE HOW BUSY HE IS!

10:22 P.M.
I guess I never write much in my journal about the good fun things. TODAY HAS BEEN GOOD AND THE REST OF MY LIFE WILL BE BETTER! I wish I could feel this up all the time.

May 25
Cam and I went to the museum after school. Loved it!

They had a visiting painters exhibition and I remembered how ever since moving to Arizona I'd always wanted to paint the red cliffs, the pink sand, the fragile little flowers under the cactus and around the big rocks. Maybe Cam and I can do it next weekend. Wouldn't that be exciting? Buying paints, hiking, being one with nature and beauty.

AND TONIGHT IS THE BARN DANCE!

May 26
12:34 A.M.
This has been one of the funnest nights of my life. I know that's not a word but I like it! The gym was decorated barnyard style. We even had a real cow and a couple of sheep and some squawking geese—in pens, of course. Everyone felt loose and loud and we had hot dogs, sloppy joes, and brownies. Everybody ate and danced and sang. Principal Loggin was dressed like an old hayseed farmer and when he

sang (unbelievably off-key) it was like the funniest thing I've ever heard or seen. Miss Johnson, the science teacher, was with him and everybody yelled and clapped and stomped their feet, as well as begged them to do more . . . and more . . . AND MORE!!!!

It was really nice of Mr. Levine (who has the biggest bank in town) to pay for the whole party. He said it was to honor all eight of his kids who had graduated from here.

I took my turn at the serving table and I don't know when I've worked harder or EATEN MORE! Tad was always with me and we lifted up the big heated units of sloppy joe mix like we were stevedores. Now my back is paying the penalty. Ouch! Ouch! and more OUCH!

12:21 P.M.

Woke up feeling as bloated as the big old black-and-white cow at the Barn Dance. Yuck! I just reached down and my belly is so extended it feels like I swallowed a watermelon. I'm repulsed! How can I overeat so much? I hate myself, I'm such a grunt, grunt hog! Thank goodness tomorrow I'm going out with Jade. She's been on our committee and she is really cool. We're going to bike up all the way to Red Ravine. That should take some blubber off.

May 30

GRADUATION! School is out for the summer. Actually, high school is OUT for the rest of our lives! I don't know if I'm sad or happy . . . I think I'm both! That probably wouldn't make sense to anyone else . . . but it does to me.

It was sheer bedlam when we were trying to put on our graduation gowns. We were all hugging and kissing and crying and laughing and teasing and joking and . . . maybe all of us feeling like we were going to get shipped off to a different planet or something.

Gregory Zetorizon gave the valedictorian address, and we were all feeling more grateful for America than we ever had been before in our lives. In fact, even the guys were trying to hold back tears. Principal Loggin was crying openly and unashamedly.

Gregory told us how his parents and grandparents had struggled to get even a meager education and some of the tragic things that had happened to them in their third world country. He stopped speaking for a moment, then almost whispered, "I love America. I feel honored to be here."

As he pulled a Kleenex out of his pocket to wipe his eyes, the student body automatically and without any encouragement at all stood and solemnly repeated, "I LOVE AMERICA. I FEEL HONORED TO BE HERE!"

It was a touching and wonderful experience that I'm sure none of us will ever forget, nor would we want to.

May 31
The Regional Gymnastics were wild, woolly, and wonderful. I think I did better than I ever have before. I hope my films

come out okay so Miss M. can send them off to UCLA . . . and . . . I can have a copy to show off to . . . nobody. I'm not really the show-off type at all.

Our school got second place, and that was after Nicole had a miserable layout and Meg Parker fell off the beam on her first routine.

I think I did pretty good . . . I hope I did. My points were high and we were second . . . But we desperately wanted first!

June 1
1:45 A.M.

I can't sleep and I CAN NO LONGER *PRETEND THAT WHAT HAPPENED LAST NIGHT AFTER THE GYMNASTICS PARTY DIDN'T HAPPEN!!!!!!!!!!!!!!!*

Once I read that if a person had a problem that was grinding away their guts they should talk about it . . . get it out in the open . . . let it go!!!!! NOT PRETEND IT HADN'T HAPPENED!

I was never going to allow myself to think of IT again but . . . I can't let go! IT won't let me let go! I'm living it over and over . . . feeling it . . . smelling it . . . being repulsed by it. I'VE TRIED TO THINK ABOUT THE WONDERFUL AND GOOD THINGS THAT HAVE HAPPENED THE LAST FEW DAYS . . . BUT THEY CAN'T COVER THE . . .

Would writing about it help?

MAYBE . . . here goes . . .

The Rosemunds had offered us their Employees' Rose Room for our gymnastics team party if we would help clean up.

Uggggh . . . I'm shivering and shaking and wondering where I would be now if it hadn't been for brave athletic Jade. I was putting things away in the broom closet after the party when Rod Mitchell came up behind me and started to push me into the closet and grope me. I tried to fight him off and when he put his hand over my mouth I bit him so hard he let me go for a second and I screamed. It was only a gurgling, gasping scream but Jade heard it, and almost immediately she was opening the door and doing her kickboxing thing. Big old Rod let go of me and nonchalantly started to leave. Jade looked him in the face and said we'd have him kicked off the boys' team if we ever heard of him messing around with any other girl. Then she almost growled, "In the meantime, maybe we'll report you to the police and your coach . . . if and when we feel like it." Rod pretended he had just been trying to scare me, and the coach and principal might have believed it . . . but Jade and I knew differently!

After he sauntered away I fell on the floor in a clump. Nothing like that had ever happened to me before. I couldn't even cry. After a second or two Jade put her arms around me and we rocked back and forth in silence. Then she whispered that a similar thing had once happened to her.

"What did you do?" I asked.

She closed her eyes and took an endlessly deep breath. Now it was my turn to hug her like I'd never let go. After a while she told me that SHE HADN'T BEEN RESCUED AS QUICKLY AS I WAS!

For a while we were as quiet as two little mice, then, as though she were talking to herself, she told me they never did find the boy. She and her mother and father decided she would feel more personally powerful if she took kickboxing and some self-defense classes.

I am soooo glad she shared that with me. Now I can never feel sorry for myself without feeling MORE sorry for her!

I knew Jade was creative and enthusiastic and nice, but it wasn't until now that I truly got to know the real her.

6:45 A.M.

I wish I could just think about the Barn Dance and our gymnastics meet and graduation and . . . all the other good things, but Rod's face and hands are always . . . I think I'll take a bus to the hospital and entertain the kids in the wards. I leave my puppets in Mom's office, and I'm pretty sure I love being with the kids even more than they enjoy having me and my puppets with them.

7:21 P.M.

The kids really restored me, helped me see that good people sometimes have bad things happen to them, and we have to live with it . . . well, THEY have to live with it! I CAN let it go! And I WILL!

June 2

I'm going to sleep over at Jade's house tomorrow. It's strange that since we have the secret she seems more like my sister than my friend. She had to tell her mother but I'll never tell my mom. It would be just too disgusting and . . . I NEVER want to talk or write or think of it ever again! In fact, as of right now I'm erasing that part of my life forever!

Maybe when we go out into the beautiful canyonland tomorrow all the bad stuff will just dissolve.

June 3

Jade just called. She has to go to the airport with her parents to pick up her uncle Chou, then they're going to their aunt Pearl's. She's as bent out of shape as I am, but her parents are very strict. I guess we're all stuck.

I'm feeling bad, sad, and put upon because I've been looking forward to this trip. I wanted to paint pictures of cactus and pink sand and fragile flowers to hang on my wall.

Now I'll have just another do-nothing day.

Maybe I'll get lucky and Tad will call me. I wonder what would happen if I called and asked him to go to the canyon? NO! I'm not the pushy type, and besides, I'd die if he said no.

June 4
7:02 A.M.

Jade called. They're home, and her parents said we could have a sleepover tonight. That is if my Mom says it's okay.

Mom said it would be okay and helped me pack my painting stuff. We will spend all day tomorrow in the desert.

What a lovely way to spend a day.

June 5

I'm depressed and totally humiliated! I don't know how I can explode into irrational and out-of-control actions! It's scary! Part of me knows and doesn't want to do it but it's as if some evil weak stranger takes over and I can't control ME anymore!

Whoa . . . whoa . . . whoa! I've got to center myself on the good stuff! OKAY! HERE GOES! This morning started out perfect. Jade and I were on our bikes, buzzing off shortly after the sun came up. Everything was pink and red and golden. Then slowly the sun began to ooze through the colored haze with muted, soft-as-kitten-fur rainbow colors. We both stumbled off our bikes and spread-eagled out on the path. It was like another world, another time, another us! I hope I never, never NEVER forget a single second of this day . . . well, at least the first part of the day.

Jade's mom had made us a lunch and it smelled like heaven when she opened the zipper bags. I felt too filled with beauty to eat so I cautiously and carefully hid my food behind rocks and in shrubs and the sand. I had a huge bottle of strawberry-flavored water, so that, and the radiance and splendor that were filling my soul, still kept me somewhat physically content.

We talked about the goofy day when we'd first met and how Jade's fantastic sense of humor had kept me from evaporating with embarrassment when I'd slipped in the busy school hallway.

I reached over and hugged her and told her how she'd saved my pitiful little person TWICE and how I'd be, through the eons, more grateful than she'd ever guess.

After a while we went on to other important things like boys and clothes and school, then drifted back to guys . . . boys . . . guys . . . like Tad. She seemed to understand.

We painted while we talked, and though neither one of us knew much about painting, we did amazing things. It was almost like we were part of the beauty and it transferred through our eyes to our hands. Or maybe we were just seeing what we wanted to see in our work.

We weren't even aware that the day had passed until we noticed that the sun had moved all the way over us and was beginning to sink in the west in another explosion of glory.

When we got to Jade's house her mom ragged us for being so late and not calling her. But how could we have called from another planet? That is exactly what it was like.

Mrs. Chen loved our paintings, and we promised next

time we went on an excursion we'd take a cell phone.

Now to the miserable, unbelievable, degrading part. I've tried to pretend it didn't happen. How could I have ever done such a dehumanizing thing?

When Jade and I came in, Mrs. Chen had a scrumptious late supper set out for the two of us. It smelled and looked so good, I could feel myself inhaling the hundreds and thousands of calories onto my already fat body, and I simply COULDN'T allow myself to do that. I couldn't break my fast. I wouldn't! While I was pushing my food around, wondering what I was going to do, Jade's mom called her to the phone and I hurriedly dashed into the kitchen and scooped my food into the garbage disposal.

In the other room I could hear Mr. and Mrs. Chen and Jade talking in Chinese and it was obvious that something was wrong. I wondered if Mrs. Chen had seen me throw the food away and she was insulted and was going to ask me to go home. Thank goodness it wasn't that! It was just that Jade's brother had wrecked his car and he'd called Jade to tell their parents. Mr. and Mrs. Chen talked in Chinese for a while and then they left to pick him up, telling us it might be late when they got back, so for us to lock the house, pull the shades, turn on the outdoor lights, and on and on. It was just like being at home.

NOW for the painful part!!!!!

Jade and I had cleaned the kitchen, then she went to take a shower while I phoned Mom to check in. While I was on the phone listening to Mom tell me about the wonderful day she had had and the fantastic shrimp dinner—my very favorite food in the whole world—she'd made, I suddenly became so hungry and faint I could hardly stand up. I hung up with Mom and as I wobbled toward a chair, I noticed the laundry room door was open and Poju's dog bowl was filled with table scrap leftovers. I automatically propelled myself toward it and on my hands and knees stuffed every scrap of food in the dog bowl into my mouth. I could feel tears of humiliation flooding down my face as I ate . . . but I COULDN'T STOP . . . I really, truly couldn't.

Suddenly I realized I could no longer hear Jade's shower water and I leapt to my feet and raced toward her bedroom. What if she had seen me? The pictures in my mind were too gruesome and disgusting to bear.

I fell on Jade's bed and cried and cried. She tried to comfort me because she thought I was in physical pain. I was . . . MENTALLY, PHYSICALLY, TORTUROUSLY REPELLED BY REPUGNANCE!!! Talk about having dropped to the lowest link on the food chain!

I think I woke up every ten minutes during the night, each time promising myself over and over that I would NEVER fast again. But can I keep that commitment . . . I . . . the weakest of all weaklings ever created? Oh, dear, dear God in heaven, will I ever be able to look in a mirror again?

June 6
2:13 A.M.

I must let this incident pass. I'VE GOT TO LET GO! I read once that we either hoard bad things and clutter up our minds with them, leaving little space for anything else, or we LET GO! Please, God, help me LET GO of this and all my other garbage thoughts.

10:15 A.M.

I got up early and I've turned over a whole new leaf in my life. I am a new, stronger, more optimistic, forgiving, IN-CONTROL person!

I'm SO glad I brought my journal. Often it's more therapeutic to write about a hurtful thing than to think about it. It's clearer and I can't waffle around it!

But—I'm still messed up.

I biked home and fixed myself a small bowl of whole wheat cereal, half an apple, a glass of milk, and a multi-vitamin. Eating properly is part of the NEW ME!

June 7

I'm busy this summer with my two junior college classes and gymnastics at JIM'S GYM. (I was extremely lucky to get into Jim's, especially lucky to be able to go three times a week.) I'm also working in the hospital children's ward Saturday mornings. It's really heartwarming to see the kids, some of them with terrible problems, perking up when they see the puppets, especially Reba Rabbit. I've had her since I was eight years old. I manipulate her up and down my arm and when she tucks her head under my jacket like she's shy, the little kids, no matter how sick they are, try to make her THEIR friend. It astounds me how they relate to her. Actually to all of the puppets, but especially to Reba. There are times when she really seems alive to me as well as to them.

June 13
Haven't written in a while because I've been too busy.
My eating has been normal.
AND I'M PROUD OF MYSELF!

June 19
Since school has been out I've put on a few pounds I've got to get rid of, but this time I'm going to do it the RIGHT WAY!

June 21, summer begins
Mom and I went to a family birthday dinner at her coworker's house. It was a long, hot, dull drive and everyone there was old, old, and older.

Just as I was beginning to lull myself into a grin-and-bear-it state, they started teasing me for eating like a bird, as they put it.

I said, "Haven't any of you heard of sloooow eaters, chewing one's food thirty times before one swallows it?"

They congratulated my ladylike manners and immediately

went back to stuffing their faces like pigs at a trough.

I could see they were watching me from the corners of their eyes, so I took the deepest breath I could and started eating like a pig myself, forcing large portions of roast beef into my mouth. It was a horrendous experience because I could hear the cow I was eating mooing mournfully. I could feel its slippery, bristly fat slipping down my throat. I could smell its warm milk—and even more strongly, I could smell its soft ploppy cow pies.

It took all the strength I had to force the still-mooing cow parts to stay down in my stomach until my plate was almost clean, then I stood up, mumbled, "'Scuse me," and stumbled toward the bathroom.

Quickly I turned on the water in both the bathtub and the sink, flushed the toilet, bent over, and, sticking out my tongue as far as I could, reached as far back in my throat as possible with my pointer finger. The first two times I just gagged. My mind and stomach and every other place in my body felt like they were against my upchucking, but I had to get rid of the mooing cow!

On the third try, I felt my stomach begin to undulate. The yuck that spewed up smelled awful and tasted foul. It slithered around the toilet rim and down one side. It didn't look like cow parts but . . . I had some insane little notion that maybe I should say a prayer or something. Could going down the toilet be like being cremated or sent off to wherever dead cows go?

Afraid someone would miss me, I desperately washed

my hands, face, and around the toilet rim. I had to get out of the bathroom before someone else waltzed in.

I'm thinking next time I'll . . . but there won't EVER be a next time! My body had a violent tremor. It's too disgusting, too horrible.

I . . .

want . . .

to . . .

die . . .

I've never said that before. Maybe I do and maybe I don't . . . All I'm sure about right now is that I need help. Please . . . please . . . somebody help me . . . PLEASE, PLEASE, PLEASE HELP ME!!!!!!!

June 25

Sometimes Dad really ticks me off. He just came home and was crabby and snotty to both Mom and me. I know he works long hours and he gets really tired but that's no reason to take it out on us like we're idiots!

I can't wait to go to college and get away from here. I envy Dara and Lara. I wish . . . but wishing doesn't do any good. I'm stuck here for endless months to come and I hate it, HATE IT! HATE IT! I WANT OUT!!!! Especially from Dad!!!!

June 26

I am totally heartbroken and disgusted with myself. How can I be such a selfish, self-centered, spoiled, obnoxious, uncaring, unappreciative person? My tears are falling like rain and I'm totally alone in the cold, cold world. I want to talk to Dara or Lara or Melanie or Jade or Mom or . . . anybody, but I have to leave the phone line open so that Mom can call.

I always check the voice mail first thing when I get home in case Mom or Dad has left a message. This afternoon I came home to a message from Mom saying my dear, dear daddy has had a mild heart attack and is in intensive care in his own hospital . . . That can't be! But it is!

7:00 P.M.

After eons of waiting Mama called and said Daddy was going to have an angiogram and that I should take a cab to the hospital. It was the scariest time of my life. The ride was endless and I thought at times that I too was about to have a heart attack.

I just got to see Daddy through the hall window and he looked as white as though he were already dead. There were people swarming around him like bees and I couldn't help but think that it was a TV sitcom. I couldn't get my brains to straighten out.

Mom was holding my hand so tight it hurt . . . but hurt good . . . I mean comfortingly.

After a little they pulled the blinds down and Mom and I stumbled back to the waiting room.

Another two or three eons passed before Dr. Blake, Daddy's friend, came out and told us we should go home, that everything was under control. He hugged us and told us he'd call if there was any change at all but he felt sure the worst was over. Then he walked us out to Mama's car.

9:17 P.M.

I should have known when Daddy was so crabby that he was sick. That wasn't like him at all. I am so, so sorry that I felt such awful things about him. I wonder if I can ever forgive myself if something bad does happen. I haven't been able to sleep and I'm deeply worried. I can hear Mom wandering around the apartment. The beautiful, warm, belonging home that she and Daddy have created for us. Maybe that's what caused his heart attack, too much pressure and work . . . and negativity from me! I'm such a blob sometimes . . . most of the time, and I'm sooooo afraid!

I just remembered once in church when the preacher said that "one can't have *faith and fear* at the same time." Is it possible that I am so consumed by FEAR that I haven't any room for FAITH in my life? I DO WANT TO HAVE FAITH THAT MY WONDROUS, PRECIOUS DADDY WON'T DIE. HE MUST NOT DIE! HE CAN'T DIE!!!

Maybe he won't die if I have enough faith. But how can I have faith when I don't truly know what it is? I wonder if Mama knows.

11:14 P.M.

Mama and I have been talking for hours, curled up together on the big comfy sofa in front of the friendly, warm fireplace. There aren't any lights on, just the glow from the logs, and it is so peaceful that I'm sure Mama was right when she said that our feeling "peaceful" is part of faith. We aren't very religious in this family but . . . I guess in a way we are too. Especially at serious times like this.

June 27
6:18 P.M.

Dr. Blake just called and said Daddy's all right, in fact he's raring to go. Dr. Blake suggested that Mama take him on a little vacation when he's feeling better. Mama's wondering where they should go.

I know this sounds selfish and self-centered but I'm wondering—what's going to happen to me? Will they let me stay here all alone? I wish they would let me stay with Lara and Dara, but . . . then again I don't want to stay with them. I want to be here! I've got to be here for Dad. I'll entertain him with my puppets. He loves my puppets.

6:49 P.M.

Staying in a hospital bed is driving Dad nutty so Mom and I took him a bunch of papers he'd wanted to get organized for years. That kind of stuff would really drive me nutty, but he was elated that at last he had time to do it. Isn't it amazing how different human beings are?

Once we got outside Dad's room and into the hall, Dr. Blake told Mom he had made an eight-day reservation at a nice quiet resort where he and his wife like to hide away when they have time.

Later, when I saw Dad he cried and apologized about being so cantankerous (I have no idea how to spell the word, but I love the way it sounds) right before his heart went ballistic (I'm not positively sure how to spell that word either; I need my computer).

I'm feeling so good inside I hardly have room to worry about what's going to happen to me while Mama and Daddy are gone.

Isn't it strange that all the time Dad was dangerously ill I always called them Mama and Daddy, like I did when I was little and completely dependent upon them? Ummm, life really is strange.

Mom and Dad seem to be completely taken care of . . . but what about me? No one has said a word about ME. Am I supposed to just dry up and disappear?

10:20 P.M.
The past few days have flashed by like minutes and yet it seems like years too. Sad at first, then happy, like today, when I had Dad to myself for hours. Just me and him in his dinky little hospital room while Mom was at work. I cut summer school and gymnastics.

Those days will always have a special place in my soul.

I love you, Dad

With all my heart

I NEVER want us

To be apart.

June 29

Mom and Dad left this morning for the Lazy Lake Resort. It's only thirty-eight miles from here and Dr. Blake says he'll pay for the whole trip if they don't like it. Dad said he hated it already and he wanted Dr. Blake's check in advance. Everybody laughed but me. I could feel my face with a smile on it but inside I was as uncomfortable as a cat caught in a dog cage.

Like it or not, I'm staying at the Blakes'!

I wanted to stay with Cam or Jade or Malanie, or even alone. After all, I am seventeen. BUT my parents are super-overprotective worriers, and with Dad being sick I have to go with their game plan! The thought is intolerable. But I have no choice.

B.J. Blake thinks he's God's gift to mankind . . . and femalekind! He is so good-looking the *girls* whistle at him and say sexy things. The thought of him taking me to summer school and bringing me back to his house after school is like a nightmare. He's eighteen and has his own car . . . throw-up time.

Mom dropped my stuff off at the Blakes' this morning, then took me to junior college, but . . . B.J. will pick me up. How am I ever . . . ever . . . ever going to handle that? What if he thinks . . . or tries to . . . or . . .

I hope Jade is home so I can talk to her about my insufferable situation. Thank goodness I brought my journal in my backpack and thank goodness we have a substitute teacher today so I can pretend to be taking notes about what she's saying.

I hope there is a lock on my bedroom door and that B.J. and I won't have to share a bathroom! If we do have to share one, I won't take a bath or wash my hair or anything else all the time I'm there.

5:45 P.M.

Cam wasn't home so I called Melanie. I told her B.J. picked me up after class, and as I walked toward his car, trying to be invisible, there were girls saying things that were totally gross. I did just what I thought I'd do. I said "Hello" and "Thank you" and I think, if it was possible, he was even more embarrassed than I was, probably because he had to chauffeur such a frumpy, infantile nobody. He has everything: looks, money, personality, a spot on the tennis team. Dragging around a yuck like me. That must be some blow to his ego.

Once in his house things got better. I HAVE A ROOM WITH A LOCK ON THE DOOR AND MY OWN BATHROOM! It's on the main floor while B.J.'s is upstairs.

The housekeeper, Mrs. Fergeson, is really nice. She teased B.J. and hugged me and told me how sorry she was about my father but how happy she was to meet me. It sounded like she really meant it. I asked if I could help her fix dinner. She said I didn't have to but I wanted to. I needed to!

June 30

Stuff has piled up on me so much in the last few days that I need to keep busy to keep from busting with pressure. Everyone keeps telling me that things will be all right with Dad, but how do they know? They don't have crystal balls or all-seeing powers any more than I do!

The Blakes' guest room is beautiful and big and fancy . . . but that doesn't make it feel friendly or belonging. It's like cold and scary with monsters under the bed and in the closet. That's how I sometimes used to feel when I was very, very little, and *it's how I feel now*: scared, lonely, and abandoned.

Just as I was about to pass out from fear I noticed that the wallpaper border was made up of little cherubs holding hands around the room. They were in such a muted color that they were hardly noticeable and yet they seemed to be surrounding and protecting me, driving all the dangerous things away! I feel safe now. But I'm still going to sleep with the lights on.

July 1

I wonder why Mama hasn't called! I'm so worried about Dad I'm about to fragment. What if he does have a setback up in the woods and dies? HE CAN'T DIE! OH, PLEASE, GOD, PLEASE, PLEASE, GOD, DON'T LET HIM DIE. I'LL DO ANYTHING! ANYTHING!

Like what?

Like pray with all my heart and soul. Honest, God, I will try to make restitution for all the bad things I've ever done and I'll try my hardest to be perfect from this moment on.

Well . . . I . . . don't think I can be perfect but I will do my very, very best. Honestly I will! I would promise it on the Bible if I was in my own home.

9:32 A.M.

Mom called and it sounds like they're having so much fun I'm jealous! I'm going to spend the day at Melanie's. Jade had to go somewhere with her parents. If I'm lucky I'll get to meet Nicky.

July 2
8:22 A.M.

Mama just called, and the sound of her voice melted all the coldness and sadness inside me. She apologized for phoning just as she knew B.J. and I would be leaving for school, and she and Daddy both told me how much they loved me and missed me and wished I was there with them.

B.J.'s honking so I gotta go. We've got to pick up some things for his mother.

5:20 P.M.

B.J. brought me home and dumped me, then went back to play tennis. I'm such a drag to everybody on Earth, or maybe I'm just negative. I remember a song Aunt Florence used to make me and my cousin Ashley sing every time we were negative to each other. We got so we could sing it in our sleep

*If you chance to meet a frown, do not let it stay;
Quickly turn it upside down, and smile that
frown away.*

I haven't thought of that song in forever. Ashley and I must have been maybe five or six years old. Yeah, we were just getting ready to start first grade.

I guess I'd better get ready to apologize to B.J. when he gets home. I'm so negative and unappreciative! BUT I CAN CHANGE! I WILL CHANGE! I'll be so positive and appreciative and smiley that he will have to see me as something more than a lump of fungus that has invaded his life.

It's strange how B.J. and I can both talk and tease with Dr. and Mrs. Blake and with Mrs. Fergeson but we can't say "duh" to each other. Isn't that the weirdest?

Well, it's going to change. When I hear him coming in the driveway I'm going to go and tell him how appreciative I am and how I know I inconvenience him—and how I'm amazed he hasn't smothered me or something!

WOW! I feel better having faced that! Now I just hope I can go through with it.

AND . . .

My day hasn't been really all that bad. Cam met me on the school front steps and couldn't wait to hear about the bathroom setup. She was as happy as I was to know I wouldn't have to take a shower just before or after him and . . . you know . . . everything, especially since now I have my period.

We giggled and talked and laughed about embarrassing incidents that COULD have happened until we were almost late for class. Cam's proud of me that I'm going to show my appreciation to B.J. Why do I treat him that way just because he's beautiful and smart and wealthy and a great player on our school's tennis team? Can I be jealous that HE'S ALL THAT and I'm a slug?

Gotta go hang by the phone as well as listen for B.J.'s car. Mom said she'd call about 5:30.

5:45 P.M.

Mom just called. It was so great and comforting to talk to her, and then Dad. I felt like I was a tiny little girl curled up in my blankey and sucking my thumb.

I hadn't been off the phone two minutes when I heard B.J.'s car. Half scared, half happy, I ran out to meet him. He looked so bewildered I started laughing. He stopped and got out and I started deluging him with gratitude for him being so nice and thoughtful to me and me being so selfish and cold-fish to him.

For a second he looked at me like I had gone nutty, then he started laughing out loud. We walked in the house together telling each other how uncomfortable we'd both been. He gave me a noogie and told me I was like his buggy little sister.

I've been thinking about it and it would be nice to have a brother. I've never had a brother and I suspect I never will . . . but it would be nice.

7:59 P.M.

At dinner B.J. and Dr. and Mrs. Blake and I, sometimes even Mrs. Fergeson, laughed and teased. It was like we were a real family.

Dr. Blake told us about a drunk who had come into the emergency room with a seriously bleeding ulcer. He'd brought his three little puppies under his coat and insisted they stay with him. They had to sedate the man to get him to let go of the puppies. Then the puppies started running up and down the halls and in and out of rooms with janitors, secretaries, nurses, and interns chasing after them. I suspect Dr. Blake made THAT GOOD STORY BETTER!!!

11:19 P.M.

After I'd done my homework I went out to sit on the front steps to watch the stars and moon and listen to the night music. There is something wondrous and soothing about nature.

I felt rather than saw B.J. walking around the corner of the house. He too loves God's creations. That made me feel good inside. We talked about how appreciative we are that we can take summer classes instead of just being bored and vegetating. Then we talked about what we were going to do with our lives. He is more firmly programmed about his future than I am . . . but guess what? He says he thinks I'm a very special girl . . . and I just lack self-confidence.

I suggested he share some of HIS SELF-CONFIDENCE with me and he almost shyly whispered that most of his was a sham.

I got the giggles about that and we started telling dumb horror stories about ourselves.

It was late, late, late when we went inside.

July 4
8:25 A.M.

I don't know what's wrong with me but for some reason I just feel sad. Maybe it's because today is Mrs. Blake's birthday. B.J. went up and gave her a big bear hug before breakfast and told her how important she was to him even though sometimes he was a pain.

They're very good to me here but somebody else's folks just can't take the place of your own, even for a short time. Actually they couldn't be better to me. I guess I'm just a jerk!

I wish I hadn't misplaced the twins' phone number. I'd call them collect.

4:55 P.M.—THE FOURTH OF JULY!!!!

I wish I was little and my parents were here and we were going to have fireworks and sparklers and all the stuff that goes with the Fourth of July. But I guess this day doesn't mean anything to the Blakes.

B.J. just drove up and we sat on the porch swing in the shade and talked about everything in creation. I'm going to miss him when my life goes back to normal. He doesn't have a girlfriend and only a few boys occasionally come banging up in their old clunkers. We talked about our parents and Mrs. Fergeson and UCLA and Stanford, where he's going.

Dr. Blake called and said he'd be home late.

9:40 P.M.

Dr. Blake came home with a big sack of fireworks stuff and we all had a TRULY WONDROUS time being patriotic.

11:31 P.M.

Only four more days and Mom and Dad will be home!

July 5
10:02 P.M.

I'm thinking about Mom and Dad calling me every night. It's really strange but I'm happy as anything when I'm talking to them and hearing about what a nice cozy lazy time they're having together, just the two of them. However, when they hang up I immediately begin to feel deeply lonely and left out, like an empty misfit. I usually cry for a while until I can get myself back together. Crazy, huh?

I'm really working hard in gymnastics and my classes. I've got to make them proud of me!

July 6
9:00 A.M.

Neither B.J. nor I had classes today and Mrs. Fergeson is taking the weekend off to visit her sister, so B.J. and I did the dishes and straightened up. After we'd finished he asked me if I'd like to have him take me somewhere. At first I said "No," then I asked him if Melanie or Jade could play tennis on his court, unless he was going to play with someone or something. At first he tried to seem macho, then he said it was okay.

10:14 P.M.

This has been a super fantastic day. B.J. and I picked up Melanie with the top down on his car. Then we came back to his house and played tennis until Melanie and I were too embarrassed to play any longer. We played Three-Way, with him playing against the two of us and beating our sox off with every game. *He's GOOD!*

Then we went swimming and played Three-Way water volleyball, with him, of course, making us look like the amateurs we are! It was funny and fun and he said he'd never let us live it down.

B.J. ordered two huge pizzas and after we'd gorged ourselves he again beat us at Donkey Tennis, but this time not as badly since it's the dumbest of all dumb games.

Late afternoon, after Melanie had called her mom, and B.J. had left a note for his mom, we went to McDonald's (more food), then to an early movie. It was as stupid as scary stupid movies get, but we had fun anyway. B.J. sat between us with a barrel of popcorn in his lap and Melanie and I grabbed fistfuls every time a scary thing happened. There were plenty of them! And we giggled until the people around us told us "Shhhh."

It was cool when we took Melanie home but we still left the top down. I think this has been the FUNNEST DAY OF MY LIFE! Would that every day could be like this! And that Jade and Cam could be with us! The only thing is: pizza . . . McDonald's . . . popcorn. I'm a pig! I *will* do better.

Melanie hated to go home early but her mom insisted. They're leaving at 5 in the morning to visit her dad's old coach, who lives almost a hundred miles away. Melanie thinks it's going to be a long old dull day.

I missed Mom and Dad's call. In fact, I'm ashamed to admit I forgot all about it. Mrs. Blake said she had a nice talk with them and they'll be home Monday. I can't wait. I can't wait! My own bed, my birds . . . it really is true that THERE'S NO PLACE LIKE HOME.

July 7, Saturday
9:45 P.M.

Slept late, then went to the country club with the Blakes. It was fun. B.J. and I watched a tennis match while his folks played golf. I bet on the tall blond guy while B.J. bet on the dark-haired one. The bet was that whoever's guy lost had to do the dinner dishes.

I wanted to yell and stand up and jump up and down I was so filled with energy and playfulness, but of course I had to restrain myself. I didn't want everybody to think I was some kind of mutant. Even more, I didn't want to have to do the dishes alone and clean up the kitchen.

After the match, which my guy lost, of course, we went to the buffet lunch. B.J.'s parents were still on the course so we ate like two starving orphans. Then B.J. dared me to eat caviar. Yuck! Uncooked fish eggs! They tasted as bad as they looked, and thank goodness we were sitting kind of behind a palm, because I really gagged. In fact, for a minute I thought I was going to throw up. Wouldn't *that* have been humiliating?

July 9, Happy Monday Morning!

I've got all my stuff packed, because . . . WHOOPIE . . . today I'm going home! I am so happy, happy, happy.

I'm going to put my things in the trunk of B.J.'s car before we go to school, and after class he'll dump me off at MY HOME. His home is nice and bigger than ours with a huge tennis court and swimming pool but . . . I think "Home is *really* where your heart is." I heard that somewhere once and I LOVE IT!

I'm so-so-so-soooo excited about seeing my precious mom and dad. How could I be so lucky to have them as parents? I'm making myself a promise right now that I'll never be rude or unkind or thoughtless or selfish or disrespectful to either one of them again, ever. I'm soooo ashamed of myself for having treated them so thoughtlessly in the past. Well, THE PAST IS IN THE PAST, and from now on I'm going to be the respectful, appreciative person I should be!

All my stuff is sitting by the front door. I've cleaned the bathroom and made the bed in the Blakes' guest room.

There will not be one single thing of me left here. I will be like a phantom who just floated through. NO! I hope I will have left a little brightness in the Blakes' lives. They certainly will have left a large, happy, and colorful place in mine.

It seems like I've been away from my real home for

months and months. Not that I haven't loved and appreciated Dr. and Mrs. Blake and Mrs. Fergeson, they're all totally wonderful people . . . and B.J. would make a *good* brother! I wish . . . but I guess my mom's too old for that.

I'm just rambling on paper because there is nothing else to do. I AM SOOOO BORED! I'm not sure I can wait till Mrs. Fergeson comes to work. Even helping her fix breakfast will be better than just waiting, waiting, waiting. Wow! I hear her car coming up the driveway.

Sweet thoughts of seeing Mom and Dad are almost more than I can bear. They love me so much and I love them even more! Nothing in my life will ever make me sad or upset again! I promise!!!

Cross my fingers

Cross my toes

Cross my eyes

And pick my nose.

Mom hates that little ditty but she always laughs when I use it.

It's going to be "heaven" to be "home" with my mom and my dad and my birds and MY EVERYTHING!

2:33 P.M.

My summer school teacher thinks I'm writing a paper on ETHICS but my brain is plugged into other more important things.

11:30 P.M.

Being in MY home with MY mom and dad is about the nicest thing in the world. THE POET WAS RIGHT! GOD IS IN HIS HEAVEN. ALL IS RIGHT IN THE WORLD.

July 10

When I came out of my room I heard Mom and Dad arguing in the kitchen. She didn't want him to go to the hospital today . . . but he was insisting that he absolutely couldn't handle just lying around anymore.

My parents don't argue that often and it scares me. I DON'T want Dad to get sick again. Please, please, Dad, don't go back to work too soon. I'm not sure I could take it if anything happened to you a second time! I crept back into my room and I want to do SOMETHING TO HELP . . . BUT WHAT?

When I finally forced myself into the kitchen it was so quiet my heart almost stopped beating . . . until I saw Mom and Dad hugging like they would never let go. I dashed over to them and we had a three-way hugging and crying circle. We're such a loony lot.

July 11

I went to JIM'S GYM thinking I was about the luckiest, happiest kid alive until . . . Jim asked me to come into his office after practice. He said he knew my dad had been ill etc., etc., etc., then he suggested I get on the scales. I couldn't believe I'd gained over SEVEN POUNDS! I wanted to drop through the floor. I knew I hadn't been at my peak, but . . . OVER SEVEN POUNDS! No wonder I'd been screwing up!! But I didn't need or deserve the lecture he gave me!!! I wanted to scream and run out of there and never EVER come back. He didn't have to rub in what a loser I was!

6:49 P.M.

I told Mom I had a headache and went straight to bed. Feeling such a failure that I wanted to disappear off the face of the earth.

Mom brought me some dinner. Thank goodness it was mainly soft stuff and I could flush it down the toilet.

7:20 P.M.

I'm going to show Jim I'm not as worthless as he thinks I am! And I absolutely am going on a water diet until I've lost at least TEN POUNDS. In fact, I think I'll go down to the exercise room in the basement right now.

9:40 P.M.

Man, what a workout! Almost two hours. I'll bet I'll sleep like a log tonight . . . that is if Coach Yuck doesn't invade my dreams.

My little guardian angel, or whatever, just fluttered into my mind. I'm soooo ashamed of thinking such negative, horrible things about Coach. He wasn't trying to cut me down or reprimand me. Actually, he was lovingly, caringly trying to help me. Jerky me—always, well, almost always, looking at the negative instead of the positive.

July 13

I've been so busy trying to help Dad, and apologizing to Coach, and helping prepare JIM'S GYM for our regional meet, that I'm about worn to a frazzle.

I'm doing pretty well with the "EATING THING" too! I'm following *The Gymnast's Guide: Eating for a Gold Medal*—no more fasting! Ever!

July 14

We won the meet by a lot of points. I had no idea we were so good. But we should be. We've got the best teacher in the world. I admire Jim, respect him, and someday want to be as perfect as he is. How lucky I am!

Isn't it strange that sometimes life is so boring and dull and slow that it doesn't seem worth living, and other times it's so busy and blissful it's almost like a dream. Like now! Summer school is out, Jim's gymnastic team took us to top ratings, and Tad's having a party on Monday.

4:33 P.M.

Tad called! He asked if I wanted to come early and help him set up. I was ecstatic!!!

GOTTA GO . . . GET READY.

11:33 P.M.

The party was fun. Tad was nice and sweet and friendly to me. I guess I have to admit that . . . I *still* have a deep crush on him. He is about everything a girl could want in a guy.

July 17

Mom came in and woke me from a deep, deep sleep. She shook my shoulder and told me Tad was on the phone. Semidazed, I said "Hi," and he started laughing with embarrassment. "I knew you'd be sleeping late. But it's almost noon."

We joked around for a few minutes, then he asked me if I'd like to ride up to the falls with him. He had to deliver a package for his father and he didn't want to go alone. "Thanks, thanks a lot," I said. "You called me after you'd gone through the whole school roster, right?" He pretended to be hurt and I apologized. He's picking me up in half an hour!

4:43 P.M.

We had a really sweet trip; the day was gorgeous, the falls, even though they are tiny, were beautiful, and we were so busy talking about the party that we were sometimes both talking at the same time.

When we were coming home and almost at the mouth of the canyon, Tad slowed down and parked in the shade of a big red overhanging cliff. "I need to talk to you, Kim," he said, like it was really serious. My first thought was to wonder what I *had done*, then I noticed that Tad was biting his lip and his hands were locked together.

We were quiet for a long time. Finally he said, "Kim, will you go with me to my father's wedding Friday?"

For what seemed a long time I couldn't say anything. I was so confused. He whispered, "It's okay, Kim, you don't have to go. I can't blame you, last minute and everything." I didn't understand why he seemed so sad.

I wanted to say something that would help him but I was afraid whatever I said would just make things worse. Finally I just said, "Tad, I wouldn't hurt you for anything. Of course I'll go."

A little sob squeaked out of him, then he started laughing. It was a wet, not-quite-happy kind of laughter, but it sort of pushed out at least some of the black cloud that was smothering us.

After a couple of minutes he relaxed and said, "It's so humiliating . . ." He shrugged. "To have your father divorce your mother and marry a girl only a few years older than you are . . ."

I tried to hold back a gasp, but it wasn't easy. "We all have to live our own lives," I said, trying to sound mature and accepting.

He reached over and hugged me. "Thank you, Kim," he said. "I couldn't possibly take someone to the wedding who probably would have said something crude or gross like—"

I interrupted, "Like it was any of their business?"

He looked at me seriously for a minute. "I'm so glad you're my friend," he said, "and something inside told me I could TRUST you."

Then he told me that his dad HAD ALMOST ORDERED HIM TO COME TO THE WEDDING while his mom had tearfully PLEADED WITH HIM *NOT TO GO*!!

He said it had been an ugly divorce and he had been caught in the middle!

Finally, Tad, with tears in his voice, said, "Dad also ORDERED me to bring a beautiful young lady with me."

I whispered, "But that doesn't mean you HAVE TO!"

Tad sighed deeply. "IT DOES if I want Dad to PAY for college. He has very vividly let me KNOW THAT!"

I couldn't understand any parent being so . . . whatever . . . but what do I know about divorce . . . me, with the ideal prototype family.

On the way home we talked about everything BUT divorce and the wedding.

As Tad parked in front of our building he said, "You don't have to go, Kim."

I squeezed even closer to him and whispered, "Yes, I do, Tad. I have to go!"

He reached over and hugged me tightly. "Thank you,

Kim." He smiled. "You're . . . He couldn't finish his sentence and drove off blowing his nose.

July 20

The wedding was big and grandiose but it didn't seem "sacred" at all like MY family weddings. The reception at the Cactus Skyroom was elegant but it too felt empty and fake.

I am sooo grateful for MY life and so sad for Tad.

Every time I close my eyes I can feel Tad's arms around me and his face close to mine. I've told Jade and Melanie and Cam as little as possible about the wedding and reception. I told Mom and Dad a little more . . . but I don't want them, in any way, to think Tad comes from a bad family.

July 21
10:00 A.M.

Mom wanted me to go with her to the market but I told her I had a lot of things I had to do here at home. THINGS LIKE WAIT, AND WAIT . . . AND DREAM . . . AND HOPE . . .

Be still my pounding heart

And eager arms

That long to hold you

See you, feel you

Share your charms

I've never felt like this before.

(BIG SECRET)

I will love you evermore!!!!!!!!

July 21
6:15 P.M.

I've been so worried about Tad that I finally had to call his house. His mother said he wasn't home but that she'd have him call me . . . I was embarrassed and hung up.

I am soooo confused. I dream of Tad every night and write poems in my Poem Book about him. Plus I relive and RELIVE our day in the canyon—and at the uncomfortable wedding and the reception, when he held me tight and didn't seem to want to let me go even for a second. I ALMOST HATE HIS PARENTS FOR THEIR DIVORCE! CAN'T THEY UNDERSTAND WHAT ANGUISH THEY ARE TORTURING HIM WITH? DON'T THEY CARE ABOUT SHATTERING HIS LIFE?

HE NEEDS THEIR LOVE.

I WISH HE KNEW HOW MUCH I LOVE HIM!!!!!!!!!!

July 22

Tad FINALLY called . . . when I wasn't home, of course! Wouldn't you know? But he said he'd call back about five.

9:10 P.M.

I've cried until my whole body is dehydrated, my eyes feel like rocks in my head and my heart is completely shattered but . . . I think I love Tad even more deeply than I did before. And I TRULY WILL LOVE HIM EVERMORE.

A SHORT LOVE LIFE

BUT ONE THAT WILL BE PART OF ME

UNTIL THE DAY I DIE.

2:27 A.M.

I'm glad Mom and Dad had a dinner they had to go to, because no way could they have understood my feelings, the pain and emptiness.

Tad picked me up and we drove to the river and sat on a bench and talked. It was like we had the whole world to ourselves. We talked about college, and how scary it was to be transferring into a semiadult sphere.

Eventually we stumbled into the divorce.

Tad shivered. His pain seemed to be smothering him.

Tenderly he held my hands and then hugged me so tightly it was almost like we were one and he would never let me go! Between sobs he told me that he could never have made it through the fiasco without my help.

I kissed him gently on the cheek and as he turned his head I felt his tears join mine. Slowly he started telling me, almost in a whisper, about how his dad had always had girlfriends and how his mom had tolerated them because he . . . in many ways . . . was an ideal dad: Little League, camping trips, fishing, always at his games, etc.

As Tad got older and understood more he began to hate his dad as much as he loved him, then hated his mother for putting up with "the crap."

"I'll help you over this, Tad," I sobbed. "I'll be everything you want me to be forever. I'll love you and help you recover from this. Together we—"

Startled, Tad jumped to his feet.

I can't write how I felt when he gently pushed me away and told me how much he appreciated me BUT . . . The look on his face was so horrifically sad that I could almost read his mind. "You're . . . gay?" I whispered.

He closed his eyes and nodded.

My whole body and soul dehydrated.

We were silent most of the way home, except for him telling me as I got out of the car how I had literally saved his life at the wedding and reception . . . how he had been seriously considering suicide because of his feeling unfaithful to his mother by doing what his dad called his duty.

DIVORCE IS . . . no words . . .

I'LL NEVER HATE POOR, LONELY TAD WHO SUFFERS INSIDE WHILE HE'S PLAYING HAPPY GUY ON THE OUTSIDE.

PRECIOUS TAD. MY ONE AND ONLY LOVE. WHAT A TRAVESTY!

July 25

I have finished my childish mourning for Tad and for me and I am stepping into young adulthood. MY PAST IS IN MY PAST AND I AM READY TO TOSS MY SILLY JOURNAL INTO THE OLD CEDAR CHEST IN THE UNDERGROUND GARAGE. THAT IS WHERE IT BELONGS.

I am really embarrassed and depressed. I don't want to commit suicide like lots of kids, but I certainly wouldn't care if I died this very minute.

GOOD-BYE, CHILDISH JOURNAL.

Love stinks!

I think I'll go feed my face. I've found that food takes care of most of my problems.

Eating for a Gold Medal is crap!

NEW START! NEW DAY!! NEW LIFE!!!

August 27, Monday

The summer has flown by quickly. Lara and Dara spent four weeks with us and we've done lots of things and gone lots of places. Mom and Dad tease us because when the three of us are together we completely revert to early childhood.

Gymnastics has been great this summer! Jim's a really strict coach, but he's wonderful and kind too. I think he's given me more self-confidence in a few months than I've ever had in my life. And when we do something dumb he doesn't make a federal case out of it.

I think I'd try any routine he suggested. He showed us some films of him when he was young and they took our breath away. He was beautiful and perfect. Then he was in an automobile accident that really wrecked his right arm. He can use that arm for many things now but no way for gymnastics. That makes us sad for him but we appreciate what it allows him to do for us. He's a GREAT guy and I'll be sorry to leave him when I go to UCLA.

I'm living with fear of strange people, in a strange place, not liking me . . . and me being a lonely outcast . . . I haven't slept a full night for weeks and I TRULY CAN'T KEEP

ANYTHING IN MY STOMACH. It's not that I'm trying to get rid of whatever I eat, it's that food no longer seems to want to STAY down, or be my friend, like in the olden days.

Mom and Dad and Jim have noticed that I'm getting skinny but the more they try to feed me the more often I have to throw up. It's pretty yucky and I've gotten so that I always carry plastic baggies in my pockets so I can squirrel off some of the garbage before it literally becomes garbage in my stomach. Once I didn't close a bag tightly and mashed potatoes and gravy and stuff soaked through my pocket and down my leg. Thank goodness I had a jacket with me.

August 29
11:29 P.M.
I've been looking back through this journal and I've decided that the B.J. thing and the Tad thing were good for both me and them. I'm sure it was part of growing up and I'm grateful to both guys, and will be forever! Now they've both gone off to college.

August 31
I'm scared. What if I don't fit in? What if no one likes me at school and I make a complete fool out of myself? I DON'T WANT TO GO! I'VE ALWAYS DEPENDED UPON MY FAMILY AND FRIENDS FOR SECURITY AND SUPPORT. AT UCLA I WILL HAVE NOBODY! I'm afraid that I've possibly made the biggest mistake of my life.

September 1

My stomach has started accepting food again. I don't know what happened there for a while . . . but at least it's over. I'd like to stay as thin as I was but Mom, Dad, and Lara and Dara were all worried, as was Jim.

Jim will always be one of the support systems in my life. I'LL DO MY VERY BEST FOR HIM in gymnastics. He said he'd keep in touch with my work at UCLA. Even writing the word gives me goose bumps on top of goose bumps.

I . . . ALMOST WISH . . . I COULD HURT MYSELF SOME WAY . . . SO I WOULDN'T HAVE TO GO!

STUPID, HUH?

September 22, Saturday

Good-bye, beautiful Arizona!

Mom and I had all kinds of problems at the airport. By the time we had gotten my baggage and stuff to a rental car, we looked and felt like street people.

At the sorority house party everyone looked like they'd just stepped out of fashion magazines. For a minute or two I thought I'd start crying, then some nice lady ran over and hugged Mom like a long-lost friend, which she was. Mrs. Lawson and Mom had been sorority sisters in this house when they were about my age; now she's on the board.

Mrs. Lawson told me wonderful stories about Mom and introduced me to lots of the girls. A few of them seemed very nice and friendly and I began to feel like maybe, after all, it might not be as bad as I had supposed.

I HOPE I'll like the sorority. Mom would be heartbroken if I didn't. To me the worst thing about sororities and fraternities is if you're accepted you're kind of like royalty or something and if you're not accepted you're a throwaway. I'm not comfortable with that. I don't know how Mom and the twins could have been comfortable with it either.

Good grief, it's 2:32 A.M. and I've just been napping and waking up while Mom is sleeping peacefully. I guess it's because I've got so much to sort out. I wish Coach Jim were here to give me a mental mantra or something I could do to sleep.

September 23, Sunday

Mom and I are staying at this nice little hotel on Santa Monica Beach today, then we're going to just drive around the area from Santa Barbara to Tijuana, Mexico. We're like two barely teenage kids playing hooky, at least till school starts in a few days.

I don't know how Mom can sleep in when there is so much to see and to do! What if I DON'T like Mom's sorority? I wonder how she will handle it . . . how degrading it will be for her! Her friend said I'd like it but . . . even with all the nice things . . . I'm scared to my bones. I think I'll go turn the shower on high and leave the bathroom door open while I flush the toilet; that should wake the sleeping dead! . . . meaning my mom!

Santa Barbara was beautiful; Tijuana was dirty and packed with bodies and donkeys for the tourists. It was unbelievably otherworldish driving down the coast near Rosa Rita Beach and watching whales out in the ocean, splashing and tossing huge towers of water into the air. I wanted to go out on one of the tourist boats but Mom said we didn't have time.

I loved Venice Beach. It was filled with little sidewalk stands that sold all sorts of—some beautiful, some strange—things. Bodybuilders were there and people on Rollerblades. Some people were drop-dead beautiful and others were so strange-looking it was almost like going to a circus or something. When we got to the Pacific Palisades I was overcome with its beauty and wonder.

Phone call!

I talked to Dad and part of me wanted to go back home!

September 26

Mom's gone and I've moved to the sorority house!

SCHOOL STARTS IN TWO DAYS!!!!

After our dinky little schools in Arizona, UCLA seems like a city of its own. I've been lost three times already. I've got a map but everything about this campus is bigger than life. I think I could starve to death looking for the cafeteria. I see other students looking as lost and unattached as I feel. A sorority sister was supposed to go with me, but she got sick at the last minute. I guess I'll eventually find my way around . . . probably by the beginning of next semester.

Just as I was beginning to think I was the biggest moron on campus, Angela, from our house, came by and offered to help me.

It took us almost two hours to cover the whole campus until I felt semicomfortable with it, then we walked down to Westwood Village and she showed me where to catch buses and which were the nice cheap places to eat and shop, etc. It would have taken me forever to find all these things out by myself.

Just as I was beginning to think maybe I'd found a friend, two girls in a car drove by, then stopped and waved at Ang to come join them. Of course she did and I was left standing ALONE again! But anyway I'd had a lovely day exploring the campus. I am soooo lucky to be here! I hope I can make good grades in this hallowed place, and make Mom and Dad proud of me.

October 1

Today our coach, Laurie Longden, introduced herself and told us something about the team, then had each one of us tell a little bit about ourselves. Most of the people seemed nice but competitive! REALLY, REALLY COMPETITIVE! I feel extremely insignificant and small-townish. I'm wondering if I should be here? Especially after I watched some of the kids work out.

October 3, Wednesday

I'm loving gymnastics more than I ever thought I could. And this seems impossibly strange, but it's like the better and more assured I become in gymnastics, the better I become in all other things: school, my attitude, my comfort level with myself and my peers, everything. Isn't that totally amazing? It's obvious that, like Laurie said, when we're *obsessed* by one thing, we can allow ourselves to become stagnated in everything else.

I AM SO, SO, SO HAPPY! I'm filled with happiness up to my eyebrows! It's what I've always wanted. Happiness! Belonging!

October 6, Saturday

Being at a university is really, really different from high school. And living with a zillion girls in a sorority is like bedlam. I love gymnastics and the equipment is unbelievable, but I still haven't found a real friend.

Maria, my roommate, seems like a professor instead of a student. She wants to go into nuclear medicine. All she does is study and go out with her handsome hunk intellectual boyfriend, who . . . I guess . . . makes me crazy because I don't have a boyfriend.

She's out now with Lawrence and I'm here feeling alone and put upon. I miss the canyonlands and rock formations that look like castles and dungeons and gigantic gnarly fingers reaching up into the skies and everything else. I miss the precious fragile little flowers and the huge, many-armed cactus. I miss Melanie, Jade, Cam, and . . . Mom. Of all of them, I miss my mom the most . . . and Dad . . . and the twins . . . and my lifesaver, brave Jade.

9:33 P.M.

I just tried to call Mom, but she's out.

I want her! I need her! I appreciate her more than I ever have! I WANT TO GO HOME AND BE A LITTLE KID AGAIN. I'M NOT READY FOR COLLEGE.

October 19, Friday

Mom's flying up for the weekend. She'll be here tonight at 7:30. Maria's nice boyfriend, Lawrence, is going to pick Mom up for me. He came over the other day when Maria wasn't here and he's a really considerate, interesting person. He knows everything about everything, even gymnastics. He's a genius! Only nineteen and already a junior. He's fascinated by DNA and cell structure and cloning. I really admire him now that I know him a little. Too bad he's taken by Maria.

October 20, Saturday

I'm sooo glad Mom is here. I need her and she needs me. Lawrence picked her up and carried her luggage and opened the car door for her and . . . he's really well-bred.

Maria is out of town and so Lawrence was free. He drove us all over and took us to an authentic little Mexican restaurant where only one person spoke English. It was fun trying to retrieve my seventh- and eighth-grade Spanish. Mom had to try, too, and we laughed and giggled and Lawrence would only help us when he absolutely had to. After eating, Lawrence took us around to see downtown Los Angeles as well as Hollywood, then to Mom's hotel.

When he said good-bye I wanted to hug him I was so grateful, but of course I didn't.

Mom said she'd had the loveliest evening she'd had in a long time. I was glad because she had looked exhausted when she got off the plane.

October 21, Sunday

The ringing phone woke Mom and me both up. It was Lawrence. He said he'd be happy to take Mom and me to the beach and to Griffith Park Zoo if we hadn't planned anything else for the day.

Mom and I were delighted. We hadn't planned a thing and the whole idea sounded like fun.

October 22, Monday

Mom's on her way home and I'm spread out on my bed reliving things. I don't know when I've had a nicer day, or when Mom and I have been closer. Lawrence was like a catalyst that made all three of us one, in sync in every way. There's something about Lawrence that's safe and dependable. It's just too bad that he's Maria's boyfriend.

10:32 P.M.

Maria just got in and the first thing she did was call Lawrence. She blabbered on forever about molecular stuff they had done at the seminar this weekend, and the brilliant professor, and . . . actually it was like a foreign language to me. Not once did she ask him what he'd done, or how he felt or anything else. She's absolutely the most self-centered, selfish person I've ever known.

Can I be jealous?

Nope!

Yep?

Hmmmm.

October 23, Tuesday

I think there must be something wrong with me mentally. I had a pretty good day, actually a really good day in gymnastics. I felt fluid on the bars and didn't make any horrendous mistakes on the floor, but on the beam I had a couple of wobbles. I guess I wasn't all that bad, though, because Coach Longden told me I was doing fine and she was glad I was on her team. My other classes seemed relatively simple, but . . . I wonder if anyone else in creation feels as lonely and unimportant as I do? It seems like the bigger the crowd of people, the more alone I feel. Why do I feel so isolated? I know, I'm psychotic! I'm plodding through life in black and white while everyone else is joyously dancing around in garish multicolors. It's painful to be away from home. Sometimes I feel so insignificant and small I'm hardly here at all.

Let's see. Count my blessings.

Two arms, two legs, two eyes, two ears, an adequate brain, and a mom who's almost perfect. I love her so much and miss her and . . . I want to go home. I want my mama!!!

October 25, Thursday

It's only 6 A.M. but I simply had to call Mom and tell her all the wondrous things I think and feel about her. We talked for about an hour, bawling our eyes out and recalling all the fantastic times we've had together, as well as the bad times we've struggled through.

It was a wonderful experience.

10:25 P.M.

I feel so good about my talk with Mom. It's like she turned off the dark, cold whatever in me and switched on a light, bright, happy-forever, burning, Arizona-colored sparkle in my heart. I am so grateful for the telephone! It's a lot more personal and warm than e-mail.

October 27, Saturday

Thank goodness the gym is open on Saturday for those of us lonely team pumpkins who don't have anything else to do.

Becca was working on her floor exercises when I walked in. She was having a little trouble with her tumbling routine, so I went over and helped her some. Her real name is Rebecca but she likes to be called Becca.

We stayed for almost three hours, me helping her and her helping me. One on one is good!

After we'd had our showers, we went to the mall and hung out. She's a really interesting person. She's from South Africa and the blackest girl I've ever met. She's drop-dead beautiful and her posture is to die for. She's tall for a gymnast and she doesn't walk; she seems to . . . I can't think of a word, except it's like her body is full of air, not heavy fat like mine. I *hope* we'll be friends! I tried to be positive and friendly and complimentary and more interested in "her wants" than "my wants" like Mom taught me, but I don't know. I'm such a blob.

6:30 P.M.

I had barely gotten in our door and put my things down when Maria asked me if I could spend the night with somebody because she wanted to have "a friend" over . . . I almost told her where she could go, then I thought maybe it was her mother . . . or . . .

What if it's Lawrence? As the gutless wonder I am, I put a few things in my backpack and, with my tail between my legs, like a whipped dog, I slithered out the door. Probably it was Lawrence!

"Thanks," I heard Maria call. I wanted to throw up on the door and leave it there or report her to our dean or something.

On the front steps, it dawned on me that I didn't have anyplace to go. I sat on the bench in the garden for a long while trying to get up the nerve to tell Maria off and to inform her there was no way in hell she was going to kick me out of my own bedroom, but of course, I didn't dare. What if Lawrence had sneaked in the back door just as I crawled out the front one? What if they were already . . .

"DON'T GO THERE!" I sputtered to myself as I wiped tears away with the back of my hand. Oh, how I wish I had taken the time to read all the house rules. Surely girls couldn't have guys in their rooms . . . at least unless . . . OR at the last minute ask moron roommates to . . . I felt, rather than heard, someone come up behind me and hoped it was Maria coming to apologize, make amends, and beg me to come back. But it wasn't; it was Dora, the biggest dork in the house.

Dora's dad was a computer titan WHO COULD BUY ANYTHING, but you'd certainly never know it from looking at the clothes she wore and her shoulders rounded and her head bowed like she couldn't believe she was a member of the human species. I guess I must have sniffed a couple of times, because quietly she sat down beside me and, putting her hand gently on mine, whispered, "It's okay, Kimberly, most of us get lonely and homesick at first. I should know, I've been in boarding schools since I was eight years old."

I looked into her face and was astounded by the beauty and compassion that was there. She really *knew* how I was feeling. Her sweet smile sent out vibes of healing and comfort as she asked me what she could do for me, almost exactly the way my mom would have done it, and I blurted out how Maria had kicked me out of my very own room, THAT I WAS PAYING FOR. Gently she pulled out her room key and handed it to me. "*Mi casa es su casa,*" she said as she picked up my bag.

I followed Dora into her room and was totally amazed by it. She didn't just have two single beds and a couple of chests and desks. She had a computer setup like nothing I had ever seen before, beautiful pictures and rugs, and in place of the second single bed she had a huge green sofa snuggling with soft pillows. Dora looked entirely out of place but she treated me like a baby sister and I LOVED IT!

October 28, Sunday
7:21 A.M.

This morning when I woke up Dora was dressed and ready to go down for breakfast. She said she was going out after eating. It was like she had retreated back into herself . . . I WONDER WHICH ONE OF US IS THE MOST WEIRD! IS EVERYONE IN THE HOUSE A LITTLE STRANGE? I know Maria and Dora are . . . and maybe me . . . but three other girls in the sorority are on the gymnastics team and they seem pretty much together. I guess I've got to learn to understand myself before I can judge others, starting with Maria.

As I think back, I have been mostly a no-confidence, let-other-people-control-and-walk-on-me type person. I need a whole set of new rules for myself and I'll start right now!

I'll walk to my room and kick Maria and WHOEVER out! BUT . . . what if it's Lawrence?

FOR A CHANGE I'M GOING TO THINK THINGS OVER CAREFULLY.

9:30 A.M.

I HAVE NEVER BEEN MORE PROUD OF MYSELF! I told Maria she would either have to shape up or move out, that she would never again try to boss or bully me, that I had half rights in everything, and that I would report her if she ever tried to break a single house rule again. Humbly she said she wouldn't (possibly because I was holding my clenched fist in front of her face).

I feel good! I am the master of my ship! The captain of my soul!

In some ways I'd like to forget this incident ever happened; in another way I hope I *never* forget how great it feels to be IN CHARGE of my life! It's invigorating, expanding, wonderful!

October 29, Monday

I went to a movie with Ray from my communications class. He's a jerk! He talked through the whole movie. Actually, he embarrassed me and upset everyone around us. On the way home he mentioned nice places he'd like to take me to . . . I think I'd rather stay home and paint my toenails black.

November 2

I see Becca often but we are always in a hurry, running to a class or something. I wish I had her for a close friend! And I'm wondering why Lawrence so suddenly tuned me out. I've tried not to obsess about him . . . BUT . . . "I'VE BEEN THERE . . . DONE THAT!" AND NO WAY DO I WANT TO "GO THERE AND DO THAT" AGAIN!!!!!!! EVER!!!!!!! Mom thinks Lawrence is still my friend. I wish!!!

I hang with some of the girls from here but I'd certainly never tell anyone that I had NEVER had a REAL boyfriend. I wonder what is wrong with me? I've had "buddies" who wanted me on their teams and stuff but . . . Maybe I'll go out of my way to make a close friend. Becca would be nice!

November 9

I have not written for a week because school and gym are filling all my time. My Spanish teacher is a tyrant! Spanish in high school was fun. We sang songs, played games, and gave speeches, sometimes even debated . . . but Dr. Gonzoles thinks we're living back in the Dark Ages and I'm almost sure his face would crack if he smiled.

9:42 P.M.

I'm still wondering why Lawrence doesn't want me as a friend and I'm trying not to obsess about it!! I guess it's a Maria thing or he was just being nice to us, or maybe he was bored . . . but it hurts . . . IT REALLY HURTS! Maybe if I didn't have such thunder thighs . . . yucky posture . . . stringy hair, etc. . . . maybe then . . . but probably not . . .

November 10
We're going to compete in a few weeks. Of course, I won't be on the first team, but it will be exciting to know I'm slowly getting there. Coach Longden is giving me the confidence and self-power to take over my own life at last!

November 11
I am totally on top of the world! Everything in life is going MY way! School is great! Gymnastics is incredible! Becca and I are becoming closer each day. She lives off campus with her parents and in many ways I'm jealous of her.

I've had my fill of sorority life. Maybe it's just being with Maria, the negative, untidy witch, that has made sorority living the pits, but whatever; I'm glad I've found my new, strong me! MAYBE I HAD TO BE HERE TO DO THAT!

November 12
Met Lawrence by accident in the library. We studied together for a while. We didn't talk a lot but he's comfortable and safe feeling. I don't know what he could ever see in Maria. Maybe it's because she's such a BRAIN and he is too. Or? I guess I'll always wonder why he was so willing to spend time with Mom and me . . . and then so abruptly . . . ooops . . . the phone . . . I hope it's Mom . . . or Lawrence.

November 13

I dreamed about Lawrence last night. Maria woke me up just as we were really getting close . . . I want him to hate her and like me . . . Isn't that stupid? I'm soooo ashamed!

November 14

Today has been an absolute zilch, nada, zero. Everything I did was wrong. I studied the wrong things in communications and probably flunked every question on the test. How could I ever have done such a stupid thing? As though that wasn't enough, I fell off the beam three times and just simply could not get my rhythm going. It was a subzero day all around.

In the dining room they had roast beef and mashed potatoes and gravy and sticky buns and custard tarts with whipped cream on them. Absolutely everything a gymnast *shouldn't* eat! I hated myself with each bite, but I ate everything in reach anyway! It was supposed to be a good-bye party for Dr. Minor.

Well, after I'd stuffed myself, I went up to our room and did the old finger-down-the-throat thing. I hate it, but I don't want to get kicked off the team. Maybe I should take a handful of flushers too. They're expensive! Especially when some of us take as many as we do. I wonder if everybody does? Of course not!

November 15

Everything is coming at once!

I'm really in a funk. I literally worked my heart out on my

SPANISH LITERATURE ASSIGNMENT and what did I get? Humiliation in front of the whole class. Doesn't Gonzoles realize that *our* best may not come up to HIS best? After all, we're young enough to be his kids and he should be teaching and helping us! He read parts of my paper—and Ted's, and Jenny's—aloud, then ripped them to shreds.

He said he wasn't going to give anyone in the class an A, maybe not even a B or C. He must have been having a bad day, because that class is filled with supersmart students!

I was so mad I didn't cry or do anything stupid. I just thanked him for his critique. I could see the blood rush to his face when I did that and he just turned and walked out into the hall.

We could feel the silence as we waited for him to come back . . . but he didn't come back. Class ended and I honestly felt sorry for him . . . taking out his . . . whatever on us. I wish that wouldn't happen in schools . . . EVER . . . but obviously it does.

November 16

I'd left a notebook on the table in the common room and when I went down to get it Jamie asked me if I'd like to walk to the convenience store a few blocks away. It was hard keeping back the delight and honor I felt. Jamie is one of the top girls on the team AND SHE ASKED ME! I felt like Princess of Fairy-Tale Land.

As Jamie and I were passing the bakery shelf on our way to the cash register, she looked longingly at the goodies and then at me. Reading her mind was as easy as reading a billboard on the highway. We each bought a half-dozen big glazed buttermilk doughnuts and a box of laxatives and snarfed down the doughnuts on our way home.

Back at the house, I stopped for a drink while Jamie went upstairs. As I walked to the fountain, my feet felt like lead and in the hall mirror my belly looked like it was popping out more grotesquely each nanosecond.

Instead of going up to my room, I dashed down to our tiny nondescript exercise area and worked out HARD for about an hour, then took half the box of laxatives, and crashed. Many times I got up during the night and emptied. Often they were burning, excruciating, cramping sessions, but I knew it was what I had to do.

I've simply got to get myself more focused, more balanced, more in charge of my own thinking and doing. How did I get sidetracked?

November 17

I'm not feeling as miserable today as I thought I would. I did my stretching exercises for ten minutes, and ate (1 egg and 1/4 glass of skim milk), and stuck two small health bars in my backpack to tide me over till dinner. I KNOW HOW TO PROTECT MY HEALTH! AND I *WILL, WILL, WILL, WILL* DO IT FOR THE REST OF MY DAYS!!! I must remember, I am the master of my ship. I am the captain of my soul!

I think Jamie is as embarrassed as I am about the doughnut thing, because she sort of ignored me today. I can understand that. She couldn't possibly abuse her body like I do mine or she wouldn't be as on top as she is. I'm going to change! I have changed!

9:13 P.M.

I'd better get down to my homework. We're having a philosophy quiz tomorrow.

11:01 P.M.

The only glitch in my life is Maria. She has an attitude and personality that could sour milk. It's really hard living with her. We've tried to change roommates, but nobody wants her . . . or maybe it's me they don't want. No! Most of the girls here are my sort of semifriends; in fact, they're having a party next Saturday night, the 24th, with some guys at a frat house and I'm invited. I'm excited, but a little scared too. That fraternity house has a rough reputation, but I guess that's college life and I can work around it.

I've wimped out of the other frat parties I've been invited to, but—naive, unsophisticated, and unworldly as I am—I guess sooner or later I'll have to take the plunge!

I'm glad I've got Becca for a friend. I mean a really close friend I can tell anything to . . . well, almost anything. We have one class together and gymnastics and we have lunch together often (like nearly every day). She wants me to come spend the weekend with her when her folks get back from San Francisco. Her dad and mom are importers. It sounds interesting.

Becca and I wish we were roommates at the house instead of Maria and me. Maria is such a negative sourpuss and so bossy! I could never confide anything and everything to her like I can to Becca. It's nice to have someone you can talk to, I mean really talk to without any reservations . . . well, some reservations (like my stupid food thing).

She'd like to live here, but she doesn't want to too. Sort of like me; I'd like to be with my family but I like living here too.

November 20
Becca is sick. I miss her!

November 21
Tomorrow is Thanksgiving. I was going home for the weekend, then the big frat thing came up and now my parents are going to spend the holiday with Dara and Lara. I'm jealous . . . but I CAN'T WIMP OUT AGAIN! What would everyone think!!!!! Why can't I make better choices and plans? I'm scared . . . scared to go . . . and scared not to . . . .

November 22, Thanksgiving
For the first time in my life, no big revolting dinner. Ate a little fruit and some crackers. I will take good care of myself. I will!

November 24

I woke up really early, excited, curious, and a little wary. Jamie has warned me that I have to be very careful. Is the party going to be like in the movies? A wild, everybody-goes-crazy orgy? I wanted to ask Jamie more about these parties, but of course I didn't. That would just let her know how naive I am . . . I wonder if I'll meet a really nice guy there? Mr. Right? I can't wait!

2:15 P.M.

Becca met me on the quad and we surmised about the frat party, but what did WE know? She's been as overprotected as I've been all my life. I promised I'd tell her every single detail on Sunday. I wish she'd been asked but I think there will be mostly sorority girls at the party.

November 25, Sunday

Becca came over late in the day and rescued me out of my dark, misty half-sleep. She sat on the side of my bed and gently rubbed the deep wrinkles out of my forehead. I felt like I was clenched up all over, both inside and outside of my body.

"Relax, Kimberly, relax, relax," she kept saying over and over. Finally I began to feel my body losing its tenseness and I opened my eyes and tried to smile.

It took me a little while to get my head together, but when I did, words and thoughts and feelings poured out of me like a cloudburst. Thank goodness Maria was spending Thanksgiving weekend with her family so I could unload my horrendously revolting frat house experience.

I told Becca how when Jamie and Lea and I sauntered into the frat house, the guys were lined up at the door checking us out like we were goodies in a candy store window. A gorgeous blond hunk, who looked like he'd just jumped off his surfboard, started toward us. I was sure he was going for Lea or Jamie, but he wasn't! He walked straight toward me and looked into my eyes like he could see right into my soul.

"You don't know how happy I am to have *you* here," he said.

The accent on "you" made warm little waves of something roll up through my body. He said his name was Mark Marin, and he led me to a sofa in the corner. He told me in detail about his life and his family and about wanting to have a stock-and-bond company like his father. He was treating me like a goddess because I'm on the gymnastics team. He said he knew Jamie and told me what a great girl she was and how he admired her.

Soft music was playing in the background and I wondered how the fraternity could have such a bad reputation. As Mark guided me over to look at the trophy cases, he put his arm around my waist and it felt comfortable, not at all pushy.

Time passed quickly and the music got louder. We had a

couple of beers. A lot of people were doing dirty dancing and acting sleazy. Mark could see that I was a little uneasy. I looked around for Jamie and Lea, but I couldn't see them in all the mess of bodies and with the lights turned down so low. I hoped they hadn't gone home without me. They promised they wouldn't. In fact, they'd said since it was my first big-time party, they'd look after me. That made me feel better and relaxed. Besides, Mark seemed like a perfect gentleman. A couple of guys got into a fight and Mark pulled me into the hall.

"You're not comfortable in this bedlam. I can tell from your body language," he said quietly. "I'm not comfortable either, but I've pledged here so I've got to stick out the year." He shook his head. "I think it's going to go by very slowly."

I patted his arm sympathetically and he pulled my head to his shoulder. I felt I'd found a new friend and it was warm and cozy.

Mark asked if I wanted to go up to his room to talk where it was quieter. I shook my head and said, "No, thanks." Jamie had told me that meant . . . you know . . .

Mark held both my hands tightly and bit his bottom lip as he whispered, "Honestly, I didn't mean . . ." He looked embarrassed, like a little confused child. "I guess I keep forgetting I'm not living in my little town of Simi Valley anymore."

I thought I saw a tear in his eye. "I wouldn't do anything to . . ." He looked so sad.

I gave him a kiss on the cheek. "It's okay. Forget it."

Mark went into the dining room to get us some punch. While he was gone, a big drunk guy waddled by and made a pass at me. I squirmed out of his grasp just as Mark came back and we walked out into a tiny grassy area behind the building.

Everything seemed so cozy and safe that I cuddled up close and asked Mark to tell me more about when he was growing up. His voice was so low and sweet that I could feel myself floating away on a squishy gray cloud.

YEAH! A squishy gray cloud *nightmare*!

I don't have any idea how long Mark and I were out in the garden or what happened. It was like the real me had just dissolved and disappeared.

Eventually in the far, far distance I could hear little streaks of Jamie's voice screaming like it was miles away. She was calling Mark horrible names and I wanted to protect him, but the dense sticky fog both inside me and surrounding me kept me imprisoned.

Momentary snatches of Jamie and Lea almost dragging me through the stickiness popped into my mind. They struggled mightily to get me into Jamie's car, because my mind and body parts didn't seem to be connected to each other. I have no memory at all of them getting me home or into bed.

I flipped out again, and when my brain did start to unscramble, Jamie was sitting on the side of the bed. From somewhere way out in space, I could hear her begging me to come out of it.

I tried to concentrate, but it was really, really hard because our words were floating out around each other and I couldn't get them to connect. They kept slipping down and dripping off the side of the bed and out of the back of my head.

Far far away, through a bunch of big thorny bushes and an alligator marsh or something, I could feel someone shaking me and asking me if Mark had raped me. That seemed so stupid. I could hear and see an orange and blue and green wavy laugh dribbling out of me sideways. I was a cartoon character and I couldn't get off the paper.

It seemed like it was days and weeks and months before I could get myself to stay in focus, even though Jamie said it was just a few hours.

Jamie and Lea both think Mark put something in my drink, but I don't! He wouldn't have! He couldn't have! . . . Or . . . Did he?

I am soooo SCARED!

I want my mama. I want her to hug me and wipe away my tears and tell me everything is going to be all right. Please, Mama, come help me.

Please, Jamie—don't leave me.

I'm mixed up. Is it today? Tomorrow? Yesterday?

I guess I slept for a little while; now I'm even more petrified, scared than ever. What if Mark did rape me? What if I have AIDS? What if I'm *pregnant*?

Why can't I remember which days are the ones when I'm supposed to be fertile? Why didn't I let Jamie take me to the hospital like she wanted to do so they could check me? I'm so dumb! Stupid! Naive! I was afraid they'd find out I was a virgin, but maybe Jamie and Lea are both virgins too. Shall I call a cab and go now? Lea said they could give me a "morning after" pill.

I THINK I'M GOING TO EXPLODE! I'VE GOT TO DO SOMETHING!!!

10:39 A.M.

Becca and I just got back from the hospital and I feel a lot better. The doctor there was a lady and she was so kind and gentle I really appreciated her. She said I was a "lucky little puppy," that my friends got to me before Mark had time to rape me. She was certain he had given me one of the "bye-bye" pills (as Jamie called them). She tried her hardest to get me to report Mark, but I'm not ready for that yet. I still can't believe it. He seemed so nice, so caring and thoughtful and sensitive. How can anyone so good be soooo evil and such a jerk! I'd like to put a sign on every window warning girls about him, but of course, I never would. I don't want anyone to know about *dumb* me!

A couple of guys got a little persistent with me in high school, but at least then I had a chance to scream and fight them off . . . this . . . it's more than terrorizing!!! Talk about taking advantage! I wonder if I'll ever be able to trust any guy ever again! It was such a shameful, gutless, humiliating experience!

I wonder if everyone in the house was snickering and making fun of me as Jamie and Lea dragged my limp dishrag body around the side of the house and into the parking lot.

What if I stumble across Mark and some of his buddies at school? Will they make fun of me in front of everybody or ignore me like I never existed?

I'm not sure I can show my face at school . . . but if I don't that will mean he's captured me and made me his prisoner for life! I WILL NOT ALLOW THAT! IF I DO MEET HIM, I'LL LOOK HIM SQUARELY IN THE EYES LIKE I AM THE *VICTOR* IN THIS ASSAULT . . . *AND I AM.* And I will never, never, ever drink anything from a glass or a bottle I haven't opened myself.

I wonder why I have to learn everything the hard way. Why couldn't I have believed what Jamie and Lea talked about on the way to the frat house? Why did I think I was such a know-it-all?

I really can't trust ANYONE! Even someone as beguiling as Mark. No! *Not all guys are slimeballs!* Tad or Lawrence would never do anything like that!

November 29

I've been trying my best to pretend that nothing happened and that I'm the same person I was before . . . but . . . Maybe if I just CONCENTRATE on the goodness in my life I'll be able to exist in the real world again.

November 30
I'm trying!

December 1
It's not as easy as I hoped it would be to let go of the Mark thing. Horrible thoughts slip in on me. How can something so *TOTALLY OVER* deflect me completely from the important things in my life? SCHOOL IS IMPORTANT! MARK IS NOT!!!

I *hate it* that Mark takes up so much space in my mind, when I really want to reserve every inch for school and gymnastics and my almost-perfect family, and Becca, and my sorority sisters. Why can't I let Mark the sleazeball crash and burn? I'm really some kind of a nutcase and I'm getting blimp-size fat again! I noticed it on my thighs and waist when I took a shower this morning. I think I hate fat second only to Mark!

I didn't do too well on the bars today because I can't seem to shut Mark's presence out. I wonder *how long* it's going to take to do that? NOT forever, I hope!

I don't seem to be able to control *my thinking* but at least I can control *my weight*! I'm going to eat only lettuce and tomatoes for two or three days and if I run for a few miles after school, that should do it. Thank goodness I'm through with the bag-in-the-pocket thing. That always completely grosses me out, it's so slimy.

I NEED SOME GOOD THOUGHTS!!!!!

Okay! I did really well on my Spanish test. I'm sure it's because Becca has taught me many wonderful things about study habits. She's so brilliant I can't believe it. It's like having my own verbal encyclopedia.

Oh, YES! And tonight we're having a State Gym Jam at the stadium to raise money for refugees. Jamie and I were both chosen to participate. It about broke my heart when Becca didn't make it. I've got to lose another couple of pounds, which will help my balance and symmetry. That shouldn't be too hard with the heavy schedule I've set up for myself. The busier my schedule, the easier it is for me to keep Mark out of my personal little sphere.

December 2, Sunday

After the meet, Jamie practically had to push me up the stairs to my room. I was so exhausted, it was a strain for both of us even to get one foot in front of the other. We had really worked our hearts out and the stadium had been filled.

I fell on the bed and Jamie went downstairs to get us some nourishment. The thought of food gagged me, but she insisted.

Mrs. Norton hadn't left yet and she fixed us a platter of stuff that would have fed six people. Jamie brought it up, ate a little, then left.

At first I just picked at the food, not really wanting it at all, then suddenly I craved it like I had never craved anything in my life and I practically dropped the fork and started stuffing food in my mouth. I AM SOOOO ASHAMED! WHY do I do things like that? It's horrifying! It's like someone else, not me, is making me do it. Could I possibly be possessed by an evil spirit or something? That's crazy! But it's the scariest thing in the world too! Like . . . sort of like having a nightmare when I'm totally absolutely awake! Oh, please, God . . . please, somebody . . . I need help!

I've been purging—and purging—and purging, and I even stuck my finger so deep in my throat I hacked up blood, which about scared me to death. I HATE THIS! Then why do I do it? I don't have the foggiest! I wish I did!

2:30 A.M.

The laxatives have begun to work and I've also upchucked until I feel like my whole body is just a shell—a fat shell—and it's hell!

December 3

I've felt pretty ratty all day and I've come to the conclusion that bingeing and purging are absolutely crazy. I've got to show more respect for my body, especially if I want to continue to be a gymnast. Even an idiot would know that what I'm doing is wrong, wrong, wrong, and stupid! stupid! stupid!

New resolution (that I am absolutely going to keep):

I *will* eat three small well-balanced meals a day.

I *will not* purge.

I *will not* use laxatives.

December 4

I've been doing really well on my NEW RESOLUTION but I'm soooo constipated I feel like I'm full of cement. What do I do now? I'd like to talk to Becca, but she'd think I was stupid and she'd be shocked out of her sensible, nice-girl head and wouldn't know what to do either. Something's got to happen soon! I wonder how long a person can go without having a bowel movement? I wonder if I should call the school nurse or . . .

8:32 P.M.

I've really hated having to go back to flushers, but after Della, our second coach, asked me why I seemed so sluggish, I knew I had to break my commitment. I'm confused! How can my life be so messed up when, in most ways, it's so good? How much am I going to have to hide from Mom? From everyone? It's like I lose all control when it comes to fat and food! That doesn't make any sense at all, because I'm usually so focused and disciplined about everything else in my life—but maybe I'm not. Probably I'm not!

I wonder if the sun really will come out tomorrow? Or if it will ever come out again?

10:40 A.M.

It's amazing what a good bowel movement will do. I was feeling so sluggish and lumpish before; now I'm feeling light and well-balanced, clean inside and not like my body is just a receptacle for rotting fetid garbage storage. I don't want the inside of my body to be just a stinking refuse sewer dump. I want it to be clean and white and sanitary. When I think of my bowels and intestines, I never want to put anything in my mouth again. The *process* from one end to the other is too gross.

December 5

I'm having a terrible time keeping food down. The very thought of garbage and . . . raw feces . . . inside me . . . is intolerable!

But somehow I've got to keep DOWN enough nourishment to keep UP in gymnastics. I certainly don't want to be kicked off the team.

December 6

I was kind of depressed yesterday but today I'm a new, happy PERSON!

And I'm getting so excited about Christmas I'm beginning to feel like the little kid I used to be! I've already got one large luggage bag filled with wrapped presents for Mom and Dad and the twins.

I was sitting on the library steps basking in the sun when someone came up behind me and put his hands over my eyes. My first thought was that it was Mark, and my heart was beating like a parade drum. When I saw that it was Lawrence, I started crying and he, not knowing what was going on in my head, sat down beside me and comfortingly hugged me. "I'm sorry, Kim," he whispered over and over, while I tried to think of something . . . anything . . . to say . . . nothing came out so we just sat there semi-cuddling for the longest. Finally he whispered, "I like you, Kimberly. I really do, and"—he hesitated—"I hope we can be friends."

I don't know when I've been happier in my life. My whole body was tingling with joy and warmth and a kind of comfort that I don't think I've ever felt before.

There are wonderful flower beds around the library stairs, and between their fragrance and the warm little sunbeams sprinkling on our faces, Lawrence and I talked like we'd been close for forever. He told me about the new project he and his professor are starting on soon. It sounds as far-out as cloning. I'm totally awed . . . and afraid of how much outside time the project is going to take and if we'll ever have any REAL TIME to be "friends." *That* is dumb and childish and pathetic!

I didn't want to say anything about Maria, but words just slipped out about how I wouldn't feel comfortable with . . . him . . . and her . . . and me . . . and how sad I'd felt after he . . . I whispered, "sort of dumped me."

Lawrence's mouth fell open, and he said that Maria had told him, the day after he'd taken Mom to the plane to go home, that I had a "tight, serious boyfriend" that I'd had since I first got here. She'd also intimated that *I* was just using him!

That made me so mad that I wanted to hurt her, but Lawrence said not to get upset because he had stopped seeing her soon after that.

We decided we'd both just ignore THAT SITUATION and go on with our lives.

I can do that! With Lawrence as my friend I CAN DO ANYTHING!

9:10 P.M.

Lawrence picked me up in the house lounge at the same time Maria was coming down the stairs. She gave us a look that would rot apples, but we didn't care. He said she went out with lots of different guys and he didn't really want to have that kind of relationship. My heart was beating so fast I thought it was going to pop out of my sweater. What did I ever do to have him like ME!

December 7

I didn't get to see Lawrence much today because he was so busy with schoolwork plus his project. He is sooooo committed and honorable about everything he does. I'm sure he would cut me off his list immediately, without a second thought, if he knew ABOUT MY DAMN FOOD THING!!! . . . I really can't control it . . . Mama . . . Mama . . . please come and wash the whole nasty food thing out of my life!!! I'm so ashamed, humiliated, pained to my very soul.

4:27 P.M.

I've been thinking about it and . . . GOOD LUCK TO ME!!!! I think I can stop NOW that I have such a powerful, honorable, honest, intellectual, self-controlled, trustworthy friend! I HONESTLY THINK I CAN!!! AND I WILL!

10:02 P.M.

Lawrence picked me up and we sat under the big rock at Castle Beach and talked and talked until we knew each other inside out. It's a safe feeling. (I told him EVERYTHING except the eating thing.)

Later we walked along the Santa Monica beach in our bare feet and played tag with the waves coming in and going out. As the sun began to set, we watched it ever so slowly squash down into the whitecapped ocean in colors from red to yellow to orange and myriads of totally unnamed shades. We held hands like neither one of us wanted to ever let go.

December 8, Saturday
7:01 A.M.

THIRTEEN DAYS TILL SCHOOL IS OUT FOR CHRISTMAS VACATION!

These last few days have been the most wonderful days in my life—and the saddest. Lawrence still likes me a lot, but around Christmas, he's going to have to leave UCLA and me, to go back to Baltimore with Dr. Lutkin. I hate that! I hate his professor! I HATE JOHNS HOPKINS AND EVERYTHING CONNECTED WITH IT! I HATE . . .

Hey, wait a minute. I've got to stop being so selfish. *THEY* ARE DOING SOMETHING TO HELP MANKIND.

I'M SOOO ASHAMED OF MY NEGATIVE THOUGHTS! What has always been MY GOAL? Being a lowly gymnast, duh! NO! Lawrence says being physically healthy is absolutely and totally necessary, and if I decide to go into a phys ed field professionally, that's a good and honorable and worthwhile thing!

Lawrence is wonderful! What can he ever see in me? Let me count my blessings. LAWRENCE, LAWRENCE, LAWRENCE, LAWRENCE . . . AND EVERYTHING ELSE IN THE WHOLE WIDE WORLD.

December 9, Sunday

Today has been heaven. Lawrence and I have been together since the sun came up. I even went with him to drop off some papers at his professor's house. Dr. Lutkin is kind and caring. No wonder Lawrence adores him. He asked us to come in for a few minutes so he could check the notes. He looks like a real absentminded professor, but he has a gentle sense of humor and an appreciation of Lawrence that makes me absolutely love him! I'll never worry about Lawrence again when they are together.

December 10
2:14 A.M.

We didn't get home until a few minutes ago. Lawrence and I had both fallen asleep in the parking lot by the Sea Lion Restaurant. It's our very most favorite place to eat while we watch the waves as they gyrate into the shore. After we'd eaten, we sat in the car and watched the surf and listened to its music and hugged and kissed until la-la-land lulled us off. I guess we were both exhausted from trying to catch up, in just a day or so, all the time we've been apart.

I had to wake up Mrs. Norton to let me in. I've got to get some sleep so I won't look like a hag when Lawrence next sees me.

December 11

Lawrence and I don't have much time together but what we do have is precious. He says he's been waiting for ME all his life.

December 12

Dr. Lutkin is trying to get everything finished so he and Lawrence can take a few days off for Christmas. It's sweet when Lawrence tells me how Mrs. Lutkin is Christian and Dr. Lutkin is Jewish yet they manage to do each of their things joyously together! They've been married for FOREVER, like my parents.

9:45 P.M.

I went down to the snack machine to get a Coke and came back with four huge cookie boxes and four Snickers bars. I've eaten them all and I feel rotten and weak.

How can I do this when I hate FAT so much? I don't think I'd do it if Lawrence had more time for me. I'm almost positive I wouldn't! AND . . . I almost hate Becca because she *definitely* is not beset by food disorders. OH! HOW I ENVY HER!

December 16

I went to Santa Barbara with Becca and her parents for the weekend. I really didn't want to go but Lawrence said he and Dr. Lutkin would probably be tending their protoplasm or whatever day and night.

I'm lonely!!!!!!!!!!!!

December 18

Everything is piling up on me. I hate Maria as a roommate. I'm just seeing Lawrence in flashes because he's so busy. I sometimes think of Lawrence and Maria's relationship and want to either die or kill her.

Not really! But it's excruciatingly painful when pictures pass through my mind of . . . Oh, I'm so dumb and naive I make myself sick.

December 19

Lawrence came by for a little while last night. He looked so haggard and tired I wanted to blame Dr. Lutkin . . . but Lawrence stopped me and said things were almost back on track.

I love that boy so much!!!!! I actually feel only part of myself when I'm not with him.

December 20

One more day and school will be OUT for CHRISTMAS VACATION. Now I'm torn to shreds. I want to be with my parents and the twins but I WANT TO BE WITH LAWRENCE TOO! And apparently Dr. Lutkin can't let him go now. It's hopelessly frustrating.

9:22 P.M.

Lawrence stopped by for what seemed like ten minutes. We sat out in his car with his head in my lap and in no time he was soundly asleep. I loved listening to his little purring snores and I even loved wiping off the dribble that oozed out of the side of his mouth. We probably would have stayed there most of the night if a fire engine hadn't come by.

It really pained me to tell him to go home, but I knew

he was so sleep- and rest-deprived that it was injurious to his health.

I hope he doesn't go to sleep at the wheel. He only lives a few blocks away, though, so I guess he's safe.

December 21

I woke up and the house was quiet and empty. Most of the girls had left right after exams ended. The only good thing about Lawrence being so busy is *that* gave me time to obsess about my finals.

I was supposed to fly home this morning but I changed my ticket till tomorrow. I CAN'T leave Lawrence NOW! I hope my parents won't hate me! I hope the twins won't think I'm a weirdo! I hope . . . I really don't know what I hope, I'm so mixed up. I told Mom I had to help a sorority sister out today, which was a big ugly lie . . . but I didn't know what else to say. And I don't know what I'm ever going to do about tomorrow.

December 22

I called the airport and changed my ticket to the 23rd, still lying to Mom about a sick sorority sister.

I was going out of my gourd with boredom when Becca called and invited me over for brunch. That was good, because Lawrence will be working with his professor. Becca's parents WANT to meet me. Please, God, don't let them think I'm a poor example, or someone they won't approve of as a friend for their daughter. I like Jamie and Lea, but Becca I LOVE! She's like family to me. I hope I'm like family to her, and I hope they won't have a lot of heavy, heavy, high-calorie food I'll have to eat to be socially correct. Just in case, I'm on a water diet before I go there. It kind of makes me feel good to go without food. I feel . . . like powerful and in control, and I can't think of anything in the world better than being a size one. But of course that will never happen because gymnasts have to have muscles.

Maybe someday after I've retired I can be as beautifully thin as I want to be.

2:24 P.M.

Becca's parents live in an apartment on Wilshire Boulevard that's like out of a spectacular movie. Mr. Bernin has an importing company and Mrs. Bernin is about the most beautiful woman I've ever seen. She's even darker than Becca and her posture is so perfect, it seems like she's floating an inch or so off the floor. She looks like a queen or a TOP, TOP model. Even her clothes seem wispy and ethereal. At first I was trying to be stiffly socially correct, but in a few minutes, both Mr. and Mrs. Bernin had me laughing and feeling comfortable.

Becca seems so ordinary—so like me—that it's hard to imagine her in that setting. She gripes and moans and groans about her parents; what they do and say and think and how they sometimes embarrass her and all that, just like me. Hmmmm . . . life is weird, isn't it?

Mrs. Bernin had a wonderful light supper—I didn't even feel horrendously guilty eating it!

10:55 P.M.

After canceling my flight and everything for Lawrence, he had to work late with Professor Lutkin. I hate it! I hate it sooo much I ate everything I could get out of the junk food machine . . . Then . . . of course . . . had to upchuck! That's totally ridiculous!

What a pig!

Practically everyone has gone home for Christmas. Some Christmas for me!!

11:01 P.M.

Lawrence FINALLY called!

This was *not* a good day for him. He told me that he and his professor have a special dispensation to go back to Johns Hopkins to work with some other scientists on their project. I'm devastated!

December 24

Lawrence got here really early, and we snuggled down on the floor by the Christmas tree. All the girls except two had gone home. With HIS company, the whole world magically changed into a fairyland. Our tree became as big and beautiful as the one in New York's Rockefeller Plaza, and the lights on it were each like twinkling *real* stars! The evergreen fragrance was so great, we were almost intoxicated by it.

After a few minutes Lawrence pulled a little box out of his pocket and handed it to me almost apologetically. "It's not much but . . ."

I stopped his words with my kiss and I could feel *my* tears running down *his* face. He started laughing like a happy five-year-old on Christmas morning. "My present's not so bad you should be crying about it."

I wiped my tears off his cheek and whispered, "It's the greatest gift anyone in creation ever received, as great as the gifts of gold, frankincense, and myrrh."

Lawrence put his hand over my hand that was holding the box. He looked deep into my eyes and said quizzically and quietly, "Did I ever tell you my dad is an atheist?"

"No," I said, feeling a dark shiver run through me. Not believing in God and Jesus on Christmas Eve seemed . . . sad . . . as anything.

"Do you . . ." Before I could finish my question, Lawrence hugged me so tightly it was like he never wanted to let go, and slowly he began to tell me things I hadn't heard before.

Lawrence's mom and dad had married when they were older, he thirty-two and she thirty-three. They were both fledgling scientists and very happy and supportive of each other. Happy, that is, until his mom got pregnant, then she had one problem after another. She died when Lawrence was five years old.

Lawrence was raised by nannies who were carefully screened by his father. They had to be zeroed in on his intellectual stimulation, and as he outgrew a nanny's ability to expand his knowledge, a new person was found. He learned to play checkers and dominoes at four and began chess and difficult card skills and memory games at six.

He had never been to a zoo or a birthday party until he was sent away to a private boys' school at eight. There he began to realize what an abnormal life he had always lived. At twelve he was sent to England for schooling, and slowly he began to relate, particularly to Howard (another shy, misplaced boy). Dame Lotta, Howard's grandmother, invited him to her country manor on holidays and it was like living in the time of King Arthur. He and Howard sneaked up the winding stone stairs to the turret and down the steep ladder to the area which had once been a dungeon. Often they got on horses and raced through the countryside yowling and yelping, pretending they were in battle with mortal enemies coming to conquer their territory and drag away their women and children.

Lawrence, who had done very little horseback riding, fell off often as they jumped ditches and over hedges, but he was lucky never to get more than bangs and bruises, most of which could be concealed.

After a short period of silence, Lawrence said quietly, "Once on the Sabbath, Howard's grandmother took us to a church service." He closed his eyes and stretched out on the floor. Looking up at the ceiling, he began to talk so softly I had to strain to hear him as he described the vaulted, golden church ceiling that was so high it seemed to pierce the sky. And the windows containing pictures in magnificent shining stained glass. Windows that told stories so gloriously that he could still see them in his mind as distinctly as he had seen them that day. He pulled me closer and told me about one particular window of Mary holding the Baby Jesus and how he had felt that his mother, had she not been so sickly, would have held him in the same loving holy way.

Suddenly he sat up and looked into my eyes. "Kim, do you . . . ?"

I sniffed, trying to keep tears back. "Yes, Lawrence, *I do* believe in Jesus, and Mary and God and . . ."

Then I opened his gift—the sweetest little necklace with *I Love You* engraved in a heart.

At that very minute the phone rang. It was Dad and he said he and Mom and Dara and Lara couldn't survive another day of the Christmas season without me. I broke down and with deep embarrassment explained what was really happening in my life.

Dad laughed and said he would purchase tickets for both me and Lawrence to come to Arizona just for today, or maybe two days, if that was possible. He said there was a plane that would leave in two hours, if we would come.

Lawrence didn't think there was any way in the world he could leave, but when he called Dr. Lutkin and told him our circumstances, the good doctor apologized, said he hadn't realized what a tyrant he'd been and that he'd find some way to "baby-sit" their cultures for at least a week.

Within minutes we were on our way to the airport. No way did we want to miss that plane!

We didn't even bother to pick up any toiletries or extra clothes. On the plane, we joked about my having to wear some of my sisters' things and him having to borrow some of Dad's stuff.

This day has been beyond description. Mom and Dad and the twins met us at the airport and Lawrence was adopted into our family instantly. Mom had told them everything I'd told her about Lawrence. Lara and Dara teased him, saying they couldn't understand how a gorgeous, brilliant hunk like him could be drawn to their buggy little sister. He smiled and said I was "perfect"!

I had told them so much about Lawrence that they treated him like he was one of us. And they forgave me for lying about my sorority sister being sick.

December 25, Christmas Day!!!!!!!!!!!

It was fun, fun, fun with all the blinds pulled down and scented candles burning and the tree lights on and Christmas music playing softly. It was a very special, sacred, and loving occasion, actually sometimes funny too. I told Mom about Lawrence's father being an atheist, and she suggested we make this his best Christmas ever, and we did!

While we were flying home, Mom, Dad, and the twins bought stuff and wrapped packages for him. He had piles of gifts. Mom even made him a batch of chocolate chip and nut cookies and packaged one or two or three in beautifully wrapped boxes to be scattered between his two good gifts as well as all his Dollar Store gifts. He had to guess what he thought was in each of his fifteen Christmas present boxes before he opened them. We all rolled on the floor with laughter while he held the cookie boxes close to his chest and wouldn't give even Mom or me a single bite. Finally when all the packages were opened, the twins and I, amid all the boxes and wrappings, held Lawrence down and each of us took a cookie from him. It was the funniest thing I've ever done in my life. Lawrence had big tears in his eyes as he told us this was the first time he'd ever had that kind of a REAL family experience.

Mom and I made a big ham-and-vegetable omelette for brunch. I ate a little. I'll fast first thing after the holiday. Lawrence insisted upon helping us do the dishes. Then all of us, like big overfed lazy cats, decided to take naps, Lawrence and I on the floor by the Christmas tree. I'd brought in two pillows from my bed and Lawrence said he was going to take his home because it smelled like me. He is soooo wonderful and he's had it so hard, well, not really hard because his dad sends him all the money he ever needs; but . . . for the first time in my life, I'm realizing how *cold* money itself really is.

After we woke up, Mom and I played Christmas carol duets on the piano, Dara and Lara played their violins, and Dad played his saxophone. Dad even found Lawrence his old guitar. It really was Christmas, especially when Dad read the Christmas story from the Bible.

This has been a glorious day! And it was wonderful when Lawrence told Mom and me how he'd always wondered what a REAL FAMILY would be like and how he NOW knew! Isn't that about the greatest compliment our family could receive?

Late this afternoon Lawrence asked me if I thought he should call his father. He didn't feel he could wish him a merry Christmas or anything like that, but something inside him felt empty and he thought maybe if they at least talked, the hole would fill in a little.

Lawrence called his dad, who was delighted to hear from him and invited him to come visit over the holidays, but Lawrence didn't know . . .

Neither Mom nor I knew what to say until he told us that he wanted . . . maybe needed . . . to go see his father but . . . he gave Mom a big hug and sort of blubbered that he didn't want to leave her . . . maybe her even more than me.

I looked shocked and felt traumatized until they both started laughing like two goons and took me into their tight little circle with hugs and kisses. Every kid, even a big kid like Lawrence, needs a mom.

December 27, Sad Thursday

Lawrence left early this morning to visit his father in San Francisco for six days. In some small childish way, I'm mad that he's taken the Christmas spirit with him. Dumb, huh?

January 1
8:20 P.M.

Our whole family was together last night. At 12:00 exactly Lawrence called and said I had to be the first person he talked to this year! He said he missed me and couldn't wait to see me.

This afternoon I got together with Cam, Melanie, and Jade. We had so much to tell each other, and we ate everything in the fridge. We were such little pigs, but it was fun to see them. I miss them!

My New Year's resolution is to be good to myself. Starting tomorrow, it's healthy food or no food. I don't want to be fat!

January 2

I had to fly back to California alone, and it was VERY LONELY!

January 3

Lawrence is excited about what his father is working on in the MATHEMATICS AND LOGIC field of science and hopes maybe HIS project will seem as exciting to his dad as it does to him.

January 6

Back in California, I drove with Becca and her folks to Santa Barbara and had a lovely lunch, then we went to Solvang to see the zillions of acres of magnificent flowers that are grown for seeds. All the Christmas things are still up and it was fun to see kids on new bikes and Rollerblades and stuff. There's even a little strip of land on the coast called THE NORTH POLE. It was exhilarating to visit, because Santa Claus and his elves were still there for us tourists. Loved it! Missed Lawrence!

Becca and I both ate like two starving refugees everyplace we stopped, but we can run it off when we get home. I'm certainly not going to . . . you know . . . anymore!

9:22 P.M.

Lawrence had left me a voice message, and I called him immediately. He's spent the whole weekend in the lab trying to give Dr. Lutkin a little time off.

He said he and his dad are more connected than they've ever been in their lives. They stayed up most of the two nights he was there talking about their scientific projects, and Lawrence said his heart almost popped with joy when his father told him for the first time (that he could ever remember) that he was proud of him.

Lawrence was really excited about having had a hands-on experience with his father's many experiments and enterprises. I'm happy for him, but . . . in a way I guess I'm actually jealous of his father. Isn't that about the most ridiculous thing ever? Yes! It is! But I missed him so much. He's kind of like my compass in a storm, my light on a dark night, my warmth in the cold . . . my everything! He's so mature and intelligent, so strong and sure of where he's going. I'm like a dumb little dinghy, bobbing on the open sea without a rudder or a sail.

I've watched television. I've read. I've tried to call Becca but no one answers. I'm bored out of my skull. The only thing that keeps me tied to Earth is Lawrence's little "I LOVE YOU" necklace that he gave me at Christmas, otherwise boring— boring—boring.

I went out and ran for a couple of miles, then came back and exercised for a while. I feel better. It's amazing what happens when you get some oxygen in your system and some blood to your brain.

January 7

After classes Jamie and I drove out to San Fernando Valley and had the best salad I've ever eaten. Hope we go there again soon. Jamie and I compared our schedules this semester. I'm going to be drowning in work. College classes are hard, and last semester I really had to work to keep my grades up! I feel like half a person, or incomplete or something without Lawrence. I hope he will get back to a normal life soon.

I can't believe this! I'd just been asleep for a little while and I woke up so hungry I wanted to clean out a bakery. Since that was out of the question, I allowed myself to go to the snack machine and almost cleaned IT out.

UGGGGH! I'M SO DISGUSTED WITH MYSELF! WHY DO I DO THIS? And now do I take flushers or do upchucking or both? I'm such a loser. Sometimes I don't even know who I am except that I'm the weakest of all the world's weak weaklings!!!!

What can Lawrence ever see in me? Or is he just being nice because he feels sorry for me? That has to be it!

Lawrence would dump me in a minute if he could see me now. Probably so would Mom and the rest of my family.

Oh tears please stop

And give my eyes a rest

My heart has drowned

And weakness huddles

Deep within my breast

I'm lost and cursed

Not blessed

Who am I?

This creature

Only fit to cry and die.

January 8
2:48 A.M.

I am *so* scared, *so* terrified that I feel like I'm silently screaming for help as loudly as I can and no one pays any attention or tries to hear me. I've taken a box of flushers *and* upchucked. I know that isn't normal in the least, and it isn't rational or logical or sensible or—I hate to even think it—sane. Please, please, God, don't let me be crazy. I try so hard to *be in control* of everything in my life. I really truly, truly do! But I can't control ANYTHING ANYMORE. It's all out to get me!

I wonder if I should dump Lawrence *before* he dumps me. I think maybe that would be easier . . . easier? It would be like ripping out my heart . . .

January 9

Lawrence is in town but of course he's in the lab. Guess I'll go run for a few miles—that always gets my positive juices flowing.

My new goal . . . exercise more! . . . eat less!

9:22 P.M.

When I got home from my run, there was an e-mail from Lawrence. He's my everything. For a change he wrote me a fairly long letter and I feel completely devastated that I'm not with him. So close and yet so far away. I hate it that he always has to be with Dr. Lutkin.

January 10

Saw Lawrence for almost half an hour, but that just makes me more needy and greedy!

He's worried about me and thinks I'm too thin—I'm worried about him and think he's too overworked! Will we ever have real time together again?

January 11

After classes, I went out bicycling with Becca. I rode her mom's bike. Then we played on the monkey rings and the cross bars in the park, and got a pretty good workout. Actually, we both wound up with a couple of bangs, but it was fun and we about laughed ourselves silly while the little kids around us watched with their mouths open. I guess to them it was sort of like going to the circus.

January 12
4:15 A.M.

SOMETHING MADE ME RUN TO THE BATHROOM TO UPCHUCK. I TRIED A COUPLE OF TIMES, but I've been so weary for a while that I literally have to *force* myself to do *everything*! The next time I tried, my throat started bleeding and it wouldn't stop. Holding a towel to my face, I screamed for Maria and by the time she got me to the emergency room the towel was almost completely soaked with blood (at least it seemed that way).

Two of the nurses were concerned about my weight but I lied and said I was just recovering from a bad case of the flu and that I was looking forward to getting my health in order and my weight back.

They wanted to call my parents but I lied again and said they were on a little holiday.

I hate lying but what else could I do?

6:10 P.M.

I've been wondering about Mom. Could she possibly have gone through stages like I am going through? Could she ever have felt like I sometimes feel? Did she like boys and they not like her? What about the sex thing? Did she wonder about "should she or shouldn't she"? Did she ever have a scary, almost-raped time in her life? What about her mom? Did Mom think Grandma *couldn't* . . . *wouldn't* understand? Have human beings changed a lot since Grandma's time?

I wouldn't want to talk to Mom about anything that would hurt her or scare her into thinking I was weird or . . . I don't really think bingeing and purging are weird . . . lots of girls do it . . . even guys . . . it's . . . everybody's doing it if they want to look good—not that I look all that good. I've always been a little, to a lot, on the porky side. It's HORRIBLE, but I handle it the best I can.

I did finally remember to thank Maria for taking me to the hospital. We still don't get along too well, but she was there when I needed her.

6:52 P.M.

I'm making a commitment! I'm going to be as understanding and tolerant of all my friends and sorority sisters as they are of me. That means I've got a long way to go, but I'll do it! Maybe not every second of every day, but I can be a lot better in that area.

11:52 P.M.

Lawrence came over and spent the evening studying and stuff, AND I AM WHOLE AGAIN! I didn't tell him about going to the hospital. I didn't want to spoil our magic time together.

January 13, Sunday

When I saw Lawrence's face I knew something was wrong. He grabbed me so tightly I could hardly breathe, and he told me he'd been on a long, long telephone conference meeting with the administrators here and back east and they have decided to send Dr. Lutkin and him to Johns Hopkins to do more work on the project *full-time*! He leaves early tomorrow morning and he has to spend tonight in the lab.

For the longest time, we clung together like two little lost babes in the woods, then he promised he'd e-mail me every night. All I could do was agree with everything he said, even though it shattered each molecule in me.

January 14, Monday
10:49 P.M.

Now that Lawrence has left I feel like a shell of a person. Will I be able to live through this? I won't see him again until spring break!

January 18

I am not purging anymore, but I'm not eating either. Even the sight of food makes me nauseous, and when I do go out to eat, I'm using the little baggie-in-the-purse trick again.

Today I fainted as I came out of English. It was the most humiliating time of my life. I don't know how long I was out, but when I opened my eyes, it seemed like the whole class was standing around me jumping up and down behind the rows of people in front. A lady and a man were trying to get me upright but my legs and arms and everything else were like wet noodles. IT WAS THE WORST! THE GREATEST INDIGNITY OF MY LIFE. I WANTED TO DIE WITH EVERY BREATH I TOOK; IN FACT, I TRIED TO STOP BREATHING, BUT I COULDN'T, SO I CLOSED MY EYES AND TRIED TO SHRINK INTO THE DEEPEST PART OF MYSELF.

In the nurse's office, it took forever for her to check my vitals, etc. After a while I was feeling pretty much myself, but weak, even though the nurse had insisted I drink a big glass of orange juice.

I couldn't believe it when someone came in with a wheelchair and took me out to an AMBULANCE. Everyone was nice but no one wanted to tell me anything. When we got to the hospital they wheeled me down an endless hall to a LOCKED DOOR with a sign PSYCHIATRIC WARD over it. The person pushing my chair pressed a bunch of buttons and slowly the door opened.

I was so scared I couldn't do anything but shake and make strange noises. I remembered once on a late-night movie I'd seen *One Flew Over the Cuckoo's Nest*, and those scenes came thundering back into my brain.

Inside my head I was calling, "MAMA, MAMA, MAAAMAAAAA!"

A pretty little blond nurse, Molly Jensen, came up and knelt beside my chair. She said the paper in her hand stated that I was suffering from dehydration.

"Why does that put me in a psychiatric ward?" I whispered.

"Because," she said, "your school nurse thought you also might have an eating disorder."

At first I denied it. Then, after they had put an intravenous tube into my arm, I quit fighting and lying.

Nurse Jensen continued to talk to me until I felt

comfortable with her. Then she informed me that some girls with eating disorders were also suicidal, and since I didn't have any close family connections in the area they didn't want to take any chances. She also told me that I'd probably be released soon if I ate the food they gave me and followed their other orders. I responded happily. I WANTED OUT OF THERE!

January 19

Mom and Dad called twice at the hospital and it's only 6:29 A.M.

I cannot believe everything that happened yesterday could have happened in ONE DAY! Passing out in the school hall and having everyone staring and talking and gossiping and . . . I wonder if I will ever in my lifetime live it down. I'll bet most of the kids thought I was drunk or stoned or who knows what. I'm thinking about actually having been in a LOCKED-UP PSYCHO WARD! I didn't see or hear anything weird or way-out while I was there, but probably everyone was medicated down to where they were drugged zombies. What could ever have been more horrifyingly scary than that?

I'm truly scared to the bone for the first time in my life. I'm supposed to eat three small meals and three smaller snacks a day, but the food nauseates me. I don't want to be fat! Each day my energy level seems to be going down, down, down, instead of up.

UCLA has lots of stairs, which used to be nothing. Now it's like climbing Mount Everest between classes.

I had to force myself to go to gymnastics practice. Coach Laurie told me how frail I looked and suggested that I go to the on-campus therapy clinic. She said she would call Dr. Susan Hala's unit immediately. In a way that made me feel bad and sad; in another way, it made me feel like she'd given me a little lifeline for at least a while till I could get myself back together, which I hope I can do . . . but I don't know . . .

I didn't go! I can't face a therapy group.

February 1

More nothing. I'm considering dropping gymnastics. I have no energy.

How can existence seem so drab and useless? I'm not at this moment contemplating suicide or dying exactly, but . . . life is endless, emptiness within everlasting emptiness.

February 10

I'm thinking about taking a psychology class next semester. The catalog says it's "(a) the science dealing with the mind and mental processes, feelings, desires, etc., (b) the science of human and animal behavior, (c) the sum of a person's actions, traits, attitudes, thoughts, etc.: as the psychology of the adolescent."

I'm so excited I haven't been able to sleep, thinking about actually being able to: control my life, my actions, my doing, my aggressions, my wimpiness, my desires, my . . .

EVERYTHING! It will change my complete existence!!! I'll no longer be on a roller coaster. I'll be . . . HEY . . . NOW I'm into wishful thinking! I'm sure some psychology classes can help me BUT THEY AREN'T MAGIC!

P.S. I'm sure Lawrence would love it if I had a complete mental MAKEOVER. I'd love it too! But I don't want him to even know about the hospital experience. I will *NEVER* talk or think about *that* again!

February 12

Lawrence has been gone for almost a month, and I promised myself I wouldn't obsess on him day and night while he was away. It's been hard, but I've survived! Barely! Thoughts of him are forever streaking back and forth in my brain and heart.

I don't feel like eating or sleeping or anything!!!

February 14, Valentine's Day

I'm so jealous of all these couples celebrating Valentine's Day. I miss you, Lawrence!

February 15

Sweet Coach Laurie is really worried about me. She told me losing weight means losing strength and vigor, which are absolutes in gymnastics, that she's been watching me slowly lose the old sparkle and bounce I used to have and she wonders what SHE can do.

I told her I'd change, and I will! She keeps harping upon how much potential I have . . . but I'm not sure about that!

February 18

I'm trying, but it seems like I'm under constant scrutiny and being batted and battered between my coach and my keepers. I try sooooo hard to please everyone and everything—people, places, even inanimate objects. I straighten plants that have been stepped on or blown over. I talk to birds and try to happily help people . . . except Maria. I haven't gotten to her yet, but I will. I SURELY WILL! I feel guilty because I haven't done it already!

I'm beginning to think maybe I should go to the therapy group after all. Maybe.

Day???????

I blacked out in Spanish. I can't understand how or why. I was just sitting there and the lights dimmed and then went out.

The next thing I knew I was in a car and then zongo . . . back in the PSYCHO WARD, with tubes in my arms and nose and someone trying to get me to answer a lot of stupid questions that didn't make sense at all.

After a few minutes I started telling them they didn't have any right to bring me here and stuff . . . then someone put a needle in my arm and I didn't give a damn what anyone did!

Day??????

Elaine, who is my therapist here, says I'm being tube fed (which is disgusting and stupid) because my weight is way below normal. (Their stupid scales say I weigh 79 pounds; that's crap.)

Elaine says in a few hours they'll take out the tubes and stuff and start me on a liquid diet and small frequent meals. They'll tell me how much I've eaten and how much I weigh, and a nurse or aide will sit with me during meals to "provide moral support," which means to make sure I eat and don't vomit. Laxatives are forbidden, and if I do throw up, they weigh *it*. That's disgusting!

Someone stays with me when I go to the toilet—that's degrading!

Elaine said that if I cooperate with the hospital staff members, they will have less need to compromise their therapeutic function by acting as a police force. HA! I DOUBT THAT!

I don't know if they've called Mom or not. I hope not!

I don't know why I didn't pay more attention to Coach Laurie when she kept telling me I was losing too much weight and that was the reason my timing was off. Around Maria and others I always wore many-layered clothes.

All I do is eat nasty liquid, or mostly squishy stuff, what seems like every few minutes. In between someone is lecturing us about things we could care less about. They are supposed to be therapy sessions, but all four of us in the group are obviously trying our best to cut THEM OUT.

As if that isn't enough, they give us papers to study so that in our next session (in what seems like ten minutes) we can discuss them.

Elaine just told me my mom would be here in a while. I about died! I don't want her to know about this horrible experience. They HAVE NO RIGHT TO . . . but I guess they do. My heart is breaking for Mom to see me here! What did she ever do to deserve a child like me?

Mom isn't here yet and we're having to suffer through "DISCUSSION 11":

"Anorexics and bulimics are socially isolated. They are aware that they have problems, but think they are the only people in the world with such problems. Their eating behavior takes up so much of their time and thoughts that there may be nothing left over for other things or other people." (HOGWASH!)

"Studies have found that bulimics and anorexics who are abusing food are at a higher risk to abuse other substances, including drugs and alcohol." (ME? THAT'S A CROCK!)

"Anorexics and bulimics both have physical symptoms that are *physiological manifestations of their disease*." (HA! HA! HA! HA! HA!)

"If one uses vomiting as a purging method, the

following symptoms and effects often include:

"Difficulty swallowing and/or retaining food.

"Swollen and/or infected salivary glands.

"Damage to the esophagus, sometimes causing pain and/or internal bleeding.

"Burst blood vessels in the eyes.

"Excessive tooth decay and loss of tooth enamel."

Then there's a whole page of what is supposed to happen if one abuses LAXATIVES: muscle cramps, stomach cramps, digestive problems, rectal bleeding, dizziness, etc., etc., etc.

What a bunch of absolute shit! NONE of it applies to me! Well, certainly not enough to make me one of the mind monkeys they're trying to experiment with!

Time? Date? Month? Year? Century?
WHEN is Mom coming to get me out of this swarming bat cage? It SEEMS like I've been here since before the world was created . . . but . . . I KNOW it's only been a few days.

I'm literally suffering in this scary ward trying to write on the back of the dumb papers they give me to study by the little light that slithers in from the hall. And I'm trying like hell to figure out how the shit I can get out of here!!!

I've thought of every avenue of escape in the book and decided on kissing all their asses. HEY, *I'VE GOTTA GET OUT OF HERE!* I DON'T USE THAT KIND OF LANGUAGE. MOM AND LAWRENCE WOULD HATE IT! I HATE IT! BUT TWO OF THE GIRLS

TALK LIKE YOU CAN'T BELIEVE AND IT SEEMS TO HELP LET OUT SOME OF THE FILTHY BLACK PRESSURE BUILDING UP INSIDE, AT LEAST IT DOES FOR ME, AND I GUESS FOR THEM . . . But I'm not going to resort to it anymore. I'm going to OUTPSYCH the system by being a model patient (prisoner) . . . an absolutely perfect, obedient clone of the establishment.

2:01 P.M.
AT LAST! At last, Mom's here!

March 11
I'm out of lockup, Mom has gone home, and I'm back to my classes today. I feel like I'm forever behind but I guess I can catch up. I haven't gone to gymnastics yet and I'll probably be so rusty they'll want to kick me off the team.

I hope that NOBODY will EVER know where I've been these last many days, ESPECIALLY LAWRENCE. He left me a gob of e-mail, and the first thing I did when I got here was to answer it . . . lying about my computer being down . . . THAT UGLY PART OF MY LIFE WILL NEVER, NEVER, NEVER BE MENTIONED AGAIN!!!!!

I hope Mom and Dad can forget it!

March 18
12:23 P.M.
I just got up and thought I had to go to the bathroom but I can't go! Constipation is still a BIG problem. Sometimes it

causes bleeding and it hurts so bad, I feel like I'm having a baby, at least I can't imagine having a baby hurting any worse. I'm taking some kind of uggy oil the hospital gave me. It's supposed to make it better, but it doesn't!

March 23
1:33 A.M.

I woke up feeling so fat and bloated that I just had to get up and get on the scales. I've gained weight (from 79 pounds in the hospital to 85 pounds now). I looked in the mirror and I still see lots of fat places on my body. Can THEY in the psycho ward be right? Am I really into misperceptions? Can it be TRUE that I really am skinny and I just see myself as fat! Fat! Fat!

3:26 A.M.

I've cried until I'm sure I'm completely dehydrated and I've come to absolutely the saddest decision in my life . . . I've *got* to dump Lawrence!!!! There's no need to try to hang on. Sooner or later he'll find out that I'm psychotic! That my mind is broken in some crazy way that can't be fixed.

If I had measles or maybe multiple sclerosis or something that horrible, they would at least be able to do SOMETHING!

Mom and Dad and the twins call me every day after classes, and Lawrence deluges me with e-mail. Of course, I tell them EVERYTHING IS FINE!

2:33 P.M.

Lawrence and I are OVER! It simply has to be! I haven't written much about it, but ever since I first met him, I've daydreamed and nightdreamed of us eventually getting together, then engaged and married . . . then with a little family . . . but of course, that could NEVER be! I've got to accept it! Crazy me having crazy kids to saddle dear, dear Lawrence with. I won't do it! I WON'T ruin his life and humiliate him with my scrambled genes or whatever.

March 24
4:13 A.M.

I just sent Lawrence an e-mail telling him I don't want to see him anymore; that my life plans have changed; that my new agenda didn't have a place in it for him. Then I thanked him for his past friendship.

My keyboard is wet with tears. I hope it doesn't rust up and burn out or explode or deflate like I feel I'm doing.

I've never felt complete excruciating pain like this before. It's horrible, but I know eventually I'll be reduced to a place without feelings of any kind. OH . . . please let it come quickly, because I'm back in school. And I will CON-CENTRATE! . . . FOCUS! . . . RETAIN! . . . ENDURE!!!

Probably NOT REALLY LIVE . . . just endure for the rest of my black lonely days here upon Earth.

10:17 P.M.

I just got an e-mail from Lawrence, but I deleted it without reading it. That was hard, hard, hard, but something that had to be done! Now that part of my life is over. I will accept my affliction and do the best I can. Probably I'm going to have to give up gymnastics.

One can't be a gymnast without the erupting energy that explodes through the rotation of vaults, balance beams, uneven bars, and floor exercises. There is absolutely NO WAY I could do any of those things competitively now. The coaches WERE right!

I'M SOOOOO . . . SOOOOO LOST!!!!!!!!!!!

PLEASE . . .

PLEASE . . .

GOD . . . HELP ME!

March 25
2:31 A.M.

I woke up with a start! It was like someone had gently tapped me on the shoulder. I KNEW I HAD TO GO BACK TO ON-CAMPUS THERAPY!

The experience was so deeply moving that I felt myself laughing and crying at the same time and there was NO DOUBT in my mind about that being the right thing to do!

I remember I turned over and immediately fell into belonging, warm, peaceful sleep.

11:24 P.M.

At 6:13 A.M. the phone started ringing off the hook. It really made me mad! I put my head under the pillows, which seemed to make it even worse. After what seemed like an eternity of earsplitting bonging, I stumbled to my desk, grabbed the menace, and mumbled, "Hello."

From nowhere Lawrence's gentle voice vibrated through my whole being. "Don't say anything. This is an EMERGENCY. I'm on a plane. Meet me at LAX, Delta Flight 1143 at 9:14 A.M. IT'S URGENT!" His voice sounded wet, and I started shaking uncontrollably. What if his father had died, or disowned him, or he'd been kicked out of school, or he'd found out he had terminal cancer or something?

I woke Maria up and asked if I could borrow her car for a couple of hours, then worked at trying to make myself as presentable as possible, all the time what-ifs bouncing around each other inside my head.

I was at the airport over an hour early because it's hard to tell about the traffic. The waiting was torturous. Mentally I saw Lawrence being pushed in a wheelchair . . . pushing his father in a wheelchair . . . all banged up from a car accident, or groveling because of some miscalculation he'd made on the project, etc. I was a basket case UNTIL . . . I SAW HIS FACE. Then the building lit up like the Fourth of July fireworks in the stadium. We ran toward each other, old-movie melodrama style, and just stood, clinging silently together.

We must have been there a long, long time, because when we finally pulled apart, all the people from that gate had left, and we were glad.

When Lawrence finally spoke, his words dropped like mountainous boulders on my heart. "When you dumped me, I thought my life was over"—he took a deep breath—"then I realized I couldn't, I WOULDN'T, let you go. EVER!"

I forgot about my two-hour car deal with Maria and we drove to our own secluded place on the beach at Castle Rock, all the time talking about the incompleteness of our lives when we are apart. After we'd cuddled into our intimate sandy little nook, Lawrence opened his heart and shared with me some lovely intimate details of his early childhood, things he'd never told me before, about his gentle, fun-loving invalid mother, who had pampered and delighted him until a week before her death. Wistfully he told me I had reminded him of his mother from the minute he had met me in Maria's room. After his mother died, his father became almost a recluse. He hired people to take care of his son physically and mentally, but no one seemed to care in the least about him emotionally or spiritually. "These were hard years," he said quietly, "years when I felt I was a misfit in society, and the saddest thing was I didn't have YOU to share my pain with!"

I started blubbering like an idiot, but I still couldn't confide in him about my . . . problem . . . if it was one. Maybe it isn't anymore! I certainly am doing better now.

After a while, Lawrence got very quiet, then he said seriously, "Now, Kim, it's time we talked about making some major changes in our lives."

I wanted to jump up and run away, bone-shatteringly fearful of all the things he probably wanted me to change— my hair, my dress, lose a little weight—fearful he'd make me explain why I wanted to break up with him.

"I can't . . . I can't," I whispered. "You shouldn't have come. You shouldn't have!"

I started to get up but he grabbed me so tightly I could hardly breathe. "NO!" he said firmly.

"Let me go," I blubbered. "Let me go."

He held me even tighter. "I'll NEVER let you go again," he said.

An insecure little sound leaked out of my mouth. "If I'm so . . . great, why do you want to change everything about me?"

"Kim, I don't want to change one single thing about you," he said. "I just want to change MANY things about US."

I was baffled.

"I want us to be committed to each other for the rest of our lives." He whispered into my ear, "I know we're too young to marry right now, but—"

I interrupted, half with disbelief, half with total amazement. "You mean YOU want ME to marry you?"

Lawrence pushed me away playfully. "Not this very minute." He laughed.

I started crying uncontrollably. I had to tell him about my problem . . . but I couldn't. I felt he wouldn't want me if he knew what a broken, uncontrolled, demolished wreck I am . . .

He just held me tight.

Then everything splashed out at once. "You'll hate me but I have to tell you. I can't eat like normal people. I binge and purge, or hide food. I use flushers . . . and I'm sure my coaches think I should be kicked off the team."

Lawrence didn't speak but just held me tighter.

Slowly I started to tell him about "the dog bowl thing" but he put his hand over my mouth. I felt that if he had any means of transportation to make an exit he would have left me sitting there alone . . . Then I realized he too was crying.

For the longest, he held me gently in his arms and rocked me back and forth like a baby. "I know, Kim. I've known about your food problem for a long, long time," he said.

When I finally quieted down he told me that one of the lady scientists he works with in Baltimore once had the same problem, and they talk about it together now.

In a way I was relieved, in another way scared in an imprisoning, demon-captured way. His friend couldn't possibly have done all the inane, insane things I have done!

March 26
2:33 A.M.

It seems like I've been writing most of the night, and I'm not quite sure yet whether I feel better or worse about our talking. I know that I should feel better than anything in the world that Lawrence wants to marry me someday but . . . I'm scared out of my skin about my not being able to handle food . . . whatever . . . and I'm not sure at all that I can control it! I know that's infantile but . . . maybe I can. At least now I have a REAL REASON to become more IN CHARGE OF MY OWN LIFE! I guess that's a good thought to go to sleep on!

One more thing! Maria isn't mad at me for keeping her car all day. She knows Lawrence has to fly back tomorrow night. NO! Tonight because it's already tomorrow . . . Oh, dear, how can I ever let him go back? I'll be sooooo empty and lonely, but if we e-mail nearly every day and phone occasionally, I guess I'll be able to exist.

10:10 P.M.

I just got back from taking Lawrence to the airport, and I can't understand how I can be so happy and so sad at the same time.

I called Mom and told her that Lawrence wants to marry me in a few years. She seemed happy. We even discussed my "eating problem" (at least a part of it). I still can't completely accept it as anorexia and/or bulimia. That's really dumb, but I guess it's me.

It's strange how I'd never been able to talk to Mom about my food thing. Now it's like having zits or something, only a big inconvenience and annoyance . . . but probably more!

Lawrence said he was going to have his friend, Dr. Elva McGuetron, call me to give me some information about how she got her "eating problem" under control. I hope, I hope! I HOPE! I can do it too. Wouldn't THAT be too wonderful for words? Maybe I will go back to the therapy group!

I want to be, I'VE GOT TO BE, EVERYTHING Lawrence deserves. Certainly not an eating-disordered psychopath! If that last sentence wasn't written in ink, I'd ERASE IT, because Lawrence said the one thing he definitely knew about an eating disorder was that IT WAS TIED IN DEEPLY WITH SELF-ESTEEM!!!!! I can't see that, but if Lala says it's so, it is! He said his mom used to call him Lala when he was little. Oh, I love that boy sooooo much. Maybe someday, in the far distant future, we'll have a little Lala of our own.

March 29

Went to on-campus therapy today with fear and trembling. In fact, at the door I almost backed out . . . then I heard laughter and music inside. There were five girls there, and two guys, which surprised me. I had no idea college guys had eating problems too.

Jamie and Lea were there! They were glad to see me and I was ecstatic to see them.

We all sat on the floor on beanbag chairs. It was so informal and unpressured even my steel-vised traumatized guts began to slowly unknot.

Dr. Hala, Susan, smiled at the circle and asked each person to tell ME one good thing about the program. It's amazing how clearly I remember what they each said:

"I hadn't realized how disrespectfully I was treating myself until I came here."

"Me too. I think most of my life I've been dwelling on my weaknesses instead of my strengths."

"Until I came here, I often thought the only thing I could control in my life WAS FOOD."

At that everyone giggled or laughed out loud, and I found myself joining them. It was weird. I had nearly always thought I WAS THE ONLY ONE IN THE WORLD WHO HAD FOOD PROBLEMS AND FELT LIKE I FELT! WHAT A RELIEF TO REALLY KNOW THAT I AM NOT ALONE! I WAS AWARE THAT OTHER PEOPLE BINGED AND PURGED A LITTLE, BUT I TOTALLY HAD NO IDEA THAT ANYONE ELSE EVER FELT THE WAY I HAD.

April 1
I can't believe what I'm learning about myself in therapy.

April 3
I used to sometimes see myself as someone I didn't know! (Someone I probably didn't want to know!) Now I'm beginning to suspect there might be a . . . somewhat nice

person inside me somewhere . . . and MAYBE . . . *I haven't been as kind and thoughtful and considerate of her as I should have been.*

April 5

Susan asked us to write down all the good things about ourselves on one sheet. Then write down all the bad things on another. She said we wouldn't have to share them with anyone if we didn't want to. But she was sure we'd learn a lot about ourselves just from doing this one exercise.

11:10 P.M.

My "good things" page was sort of short and blah.

My "bad things" pages could go on forever!

I've read the two books Susan loaned me and I pretty much fill all the negative categories, well . . . almost.

1. TO MOST PEOPLE I GUESS I SEEM NORMAL . . . BUT THOSE PEOPLE DON'T KNOW I'VE GOT GOODIES STASHED IN MY CLOSET AND DRAWERS AND UNDER MY BED, ETC.
2. I USE FLUSHERS AND VOMIT SOMETIMES UNTIL I GET LIGHT-HEADED.
3. I THINK PESSIMISTIC THOUGHTS ABOUT FOOD! THEN EAT IT BECAUSE IT NUMBS PAIN! SHAME! AND GUILT!
4. FOOD FILLS MY UNANSWERED NEEDS AND DESIRES.
5. I SPEND EXTREME AMOUNTS OF MONEY ON FOOD AND LAXATIVES.

6. I'M INTO LIES AND DECEPTION ABOUT MY "EATING PROBLEM."

7. MY FOCUS ON BEING THIN MAKES ME OBSESS ON FOOD.

8. I PRETEND THINGS ARE OKAY WHEN THEY ARE NOT OKAY!

9. I USUALLY FEEL LIKE I DON'T REALLY HAVE A SUPPORT SYSTEM.

10. I EAT TO FIND COMFORT AND SAFETY. FOOD FILLS UP THE HOLES IN MY LIFE.

11. I LOOK FOR ESCAPE ROUTES. I AM NOT SECURE. I AM AFRAID OF CHANGES.

12. I AM NOT PREPARED TO FACE MY OWN SEXUALITY.

13. I SOMETIMES PRACTICE SELF-STARVATION UNTIL MY MENSTRUAL PERIODS STOP.

14. I CAN'T CONTROL MY IMPULSE TO EAT.

15. I KNOW MY BINGE-PURGE SYNDROMES ARE EMOTIONAL, NOT PHYSICAL!

16. I WANT TO BE NEEDED, NOTICED, SUCCESSFUL . . . TO HAVE RIGHTS AND WISHES OF MY OWN.

April 8
9:42 P.M.

Susan said we didn't have to share the good and bad things about ourselves, but we did! And it was really strange that most of us were much alike in our thinking and desires to be perfect . . . well, close to perfect.

I was totally amazed to find out that even Jamie and Lea had some of my problems. I thought THEY were faultless!!!! Especially Jamie. I will forever and ever be grateful for this therapy group!

I want to call Mom and Dad and Lawrence and the twins, this very minute . . . but maybe I'd better wait a few more weeks until I have a much better foundation!

April 10

I am so privileged to be a part of Susan's group I can hardly contain my joy.

Today Susan reminded us that "eating disorders" are a cultural phenomenon, a social problem, and an emotional condition. They can be *blamed* upon lack of love, time, and attention; lack of security; abuse; and hundreds of other things. BUT BLAME IS NOT A HEALING INFLUENCE!

For a long time we talked about what would be the greatest healing influence and finally decided upon LOVE, CONFIDENCE, SELF-TRUST, SELF-RELIANCE, COURAGE, HOPE, AND FAITH!

April 11

Mom and Dad are coming for the weekend. They will be here Friday afternoon AND THEY WILL MEET THE NEW ME! Do you think they will see any change? I hope so! I'm working hard at it, and some of my teachers have seen a difference, especially Coach Laurie! I'm still not back to my old abilities . . . but I'm getting there.

April 15

Mom and I took Dad to all the places we visited when she was here. We were like three little kids playing hooky and it was FUN! FUN! FUN!

April 16

LAWRENCE JUST CALLED TO SAY THEIR PROJECT IS *FINISHED* AND APPROVED.

HE'LL BE BACK AT UCLA BEFORE NEXT WEEKEND. POSSIBLY FOR GOOD!!!!!!

BE STILL MY WOUND-UP HEART!

April 17

Tonight Susan talked about FAITH. She said we had a lot more than we thought we had.

She asked:

Did we have faith that a green light would get us safely through an intersection?

That the water from our taps wouldn't poison us?

That our parents wouldn't toss us out on the streets? Etc., etc.

Ummmmmmm . . . I think we all knew what she was suggesting, but she didn't beat us over the head with the idea. I could feel that our circle was becoming tighter, warmer, more compassionate, more understanding, more forgiving, more everything kind and warm and uplifting! Each of us decided we didn't have it so bad . . . at least NOW that we had BEGUN to see things in their true light!!!

April 20

Lawrence is back! He says he thinks I am beginning to have more confidence in myself and my abilities. That I'm more at ease with people and on and on. I hope he's right and not just seeing what he wants to see!

He is the center of my life and my foundation!

April 30

It's strange that in the last few weeks I've not only begun to feel more comfortable with my NOT-PERFECT SELF but I've also accepted that I DON"T HAVE TO BE PERFECT!!!!!!!!!!!!!

May 2

I'm liking school a lot more. It's hard to catch up, but I relate to, admire, and respect all of my teachers . . . well, maybe not quite all. Professor Steenweig is so boring that even the flies fall off the walls. Hey, his class is required, so I guess

I'd better look for something good in it! My grades have really suffered because of everything that's happened this semester, so I'm going to summer school classes near home for some extra credits.

May 7
Another inspirational therapy class!

May 10
I loved therapy tonight. I truly believe if I had had this kind of help when I was in middle school or high school I would have patterned away from anorexia and wouldn't have had eating problems.

Susan told me I could probably be her assistant when I come back to UCLA in the fall. Isn't that exciting? Oh, and she said if I EVER feel I'm falling to call her instantly on her cell phone. What a friend!

May 21
THIS IS ONE OF THE *SADDEST YET HAPPIEST* DAYS OF MY LIFE!

Today I received my BIRTHDAY PRESENT BOX from Dad and Mom, and among the things in it was my old (not-quite-grown-up) journal. I've spent the whole night reading and rereading it . . . recalling all the good and the BAD!

I'm grateful Dad left the lock on it, because it would break his heart to know some of my monstrously stupid mistakes. With my heart almost breaking, I recalled the long-ago night when Dad caught me doing the finger-down-the-throat thing, and took me into his office and give me his A-to-Z medical lecture. I'm crying buckets of tears as I think how at that moment, I thought I hated Dad and everybody else. How stupid to suppose I was just doing things to please them!

I used to think that my THINNESS was the only thing I could CONTROL! Now I know that the eating thing, and the losing weight thing, I planted and nurtured by myself.

How did it take so many years for me to come to my senses? To stop hating myself?

MY SECRET

For the first time since I was little:

I feel good.

I feel "right."

It might take a long time to completely HEAL

BUT . . .

With the help of Mom, Dad, Lawrence, the twins, Susan, and my friends, I can do it!

HOW CAN THE AVERAGE PERSON FIND HELP FOR AN EATING PROBLEM?

There are two kinds of eating problems, overeating and undereating. In America today, the greatest problem is obesity. Anyone having problems with overeating or undereating can contact Overeaters Anonymous on the web at **www.overeatersanonymous.org**; by calling 1-505-891-2664; or by writing to Overeaters Anonymous, P.O. Box 44020, Rio Rancho, New Mexico, 87174-4020. They can receive information and remain completely anonymous. Overeaters Anonymous has more than 7,500 groups in more than 50 countries. There are no fees or dues and no membership lists are kept. The only requirement is a desire to stop eating compulsively. You can also find the locations of meetings in your town by looking in your local yellow pages.

Where else can you go for information?

- ANAD (National Association of Anorexia Nervosa and Associated Disorders)—All services are free. For information write to ANAD, P.O. Box 7, Highland Park, Illinois, 60035; call 1-847-831-3438; or visit ANAD on the web at **www.anad.org**. The association offers hotline counseling, makes referrals to support groups and other services, and publishes a newsletter and educational material.

- ANRED (Anorexia Nervosa and Related Eating Disorders, Inc.) and NEDA (National Eating Disorders Association)—For information call 1-800-931-2237. Also, you can visit ANRED on the web at **www.anred.com**, and NEDA at **www.nationaleatingdisorders.org**.

Warning Signs for Eating Disorders
Anorexia Nervosa
- Deliberate self-starvation with weight loss
- Intense, persistent fear of gaining weight
- Refusal to eat, except in tiny portions
- Continuous dieting
- Denial of hunger
- Compulsive exercising
- Excessive facial/body hair because of inadequate protein in diet
- Abnormal weight loss
- Sensitivity to cold
- Absent or irregular menstruation
- Hair loss

Bulimia Nervosa
- Preoccupation with food
- Binge eating, usually in secret
- Vomiting after binging
- Abuse of laxatives, diuretics, diet pills, or drugs to induce vomiting
- Compulsive exercising
- Swollen salivary glands
- Broken blood vessels in the eyes

Physical Repercussions from One or Both Diseases
- Malnutrition
- Intestinal ulcers
- Dehydration
- Serious heart, kidney, and liver damage
- Ruptured stomach
- Tooth/gum erosion
- Tears in the esophagus (the tube that propels food to the stomach from the throat)

Psychological Repercussions from Both Diseases
- Depression
- Low self-esteem
- Impaired family, social relationships
- Shame and guilt
- Withdrawal
- "All or nothing" thinking
- Mood swings
- A need to achieve perfection